David J Dawkins is a chef, a glass and a ceramic artist. He has serious concerns about climate change and the loss of our natural world.

This book is the first one of a series of books about the adventures of *The Six Macs*. In each book there is an environmental message. In the 5th book *The Six Macs* become eco-warriors. I think these books are my contribution towards the fight against the way we are treating our world.

The messages in the books are very light, making my books fun to read.

– David J Dawkins

David J Dawkins

THE SIX MACS AND THE SLIME MONSTER FROM LOCH NESS

AUSTIN MACAULEY PUBLISHERS™

LONDON • CAMBRIDGE • NEW YORK • SHARJAH

A CIP catalogue record for this title is available from the British Library.

ISBN 9781398437098 (Paperback)
ISBN 9781398437104 (ePub e-book)

www.austinmacauley.com

First Published 2022
Austin Macauley Publishers Ltd®
1 Canada Square
Canary Wharf
London
E14 5AA

1. Scruffy MacTuffy
2. Chaffy Mactaffy
3. Broozer Macdoozer
4. Flyer MacHigher
5. Prancer MacDancer
6. Maltliquor MacSnigger

1. The Six Macs

Scruffy MacTuffy felt his legs slithering down the Loch Ness monster's throat touching its tonsils with his feet, which were warm and slimy. He felt its teeth digging into his chest piercing his skin. "ARRRRRRRH," he shouted as he fell out of bed bumping his head on the small table.

"Arrrrrh, Arrrr, ow, ow, ow. Where am I? Where is the monster? Ooow, oh, thank you! Oooh, thank you! It was only a dream. It seemed so real," he said while rubbing his sore head.

"Ow that huuurt,"

He sat on the green-carpeted warm floor leaning up against his iron bed just to get back his bearings from where he was, to where he is. He then started to get dressed picking up his clothes from the floor that he wore last night.

Scruffy MacTuffy loves Saturday mornings, he meets up with his mates, who are the coolest gang around. They only meet at weekends, and on holidays because they go to different schools. They have a ritual whenever they meet. They touch fists and shout, 'The Six Macs.' They normally meet in their camp down by the old tip just outside town, a fifteen-minute cycle ride away. Scruffy MacTuffy always looks only partially dressed or wears a dirty shirt from the day before, and always has a never washed smell about him with nasty bad breath from not brushing his teeth. He has shoulder-length curly blonde hair which always looks a bit greasy. His hair looks a bit like his dad's, his tummy is bigger than his mate's tummies and he has quite a spotty face. His mum said it's something to do with his age.

He was just about to jump on his bike when his smartphone started to vibrate in his pocket. He pulled it from his trouser pocket, which was a bit too small for his phone. He nearly missed the call while struggling to pull his smartphone out.

"Hi, Chaffy. How are you?" asked Scruffy.

"I'm fine," replied Chaffy.

"We have all decided to go fishing today, so bring your fishing rod with you. Bring some sandwiches for lunch and cake if you can get it."

"That's great! My dad bought me a new rod and the coolest fishing reel you have ever seen for my birthday last week. The fishing rod is really long, two and a half metres. I'll be able to get right over the other side of the river," gasped Scruffy after just running up the stairs.

There were six of them in their gang. Scruffy was the only one who supplied them with cakes because his dad owns a bakery and normally brings unsold cakes home with him. He looked in the cake box, but it was empty meaning his dad had been very busy in his shop and must have sold them all.

So, he grabbed a couple of white rolls out of the bread bin and some slices of his mum's best ham from the fridge. Stuffing as much of the ham as he could into the roll, he added three large spoons of his mum's home-made brown pickle covering the ham and spilling out all over the floor.

He could not find anything to wrap the ham rolls in, so he put them into a plastic carrier bag. He tied the two plastic handles together, so the sandwich wouldn't fall out. He then tied his fishing rod to his bike and put the plastic bag with his ham rolls into his fishing bag. He jumped on his bike. It was all downhill for half the journey. Then, a steep uphill peddle which puffed him out because he was slightly overweight probably from eating too many cakes.

When he arrived, all of his mates were waiting for him with their fishing rods and sandwiches. They call themselves The Six Mac's because all of their second names begin with Mac, but they were not their real names. They made them up one rainy Sunday afternoon about two years ago just for fun. Now there made up names have stuck with them. They matched their names to their personalities because they all lived in Scotland not too far away from where the Loch Ness monster has been spotted. They thought all of their second names should begin with Mac. They also decided always to wear something tartan like a true Scotsman. Three of them always wear a tartan red scarf even in the summer, Prancer MacDancer wear a red tartan kilt most of the time and Flyer MacHigher wears a red tartan hat with a shamrock badge.

"Hi Scruffy. What happened to your head? That's quite a lump?" asked Flyer.

"I fell out of bed this morning. I was having a dream about being eaten alive by the Loch Ness monster. The dream seemed so real. It was as if it was really happening. It was so scary!" exclaimed Scruffy.

"'Ave you brought the cake?" asked Broozer Macdoozer, who was always up for a fight.

"No, sorry guys my dad must have had a busy day at his shop, and he must had sold all of the cakes," answered Scruffy.

"Hey guys, do you want to put your sandwiches in my fishing bag? They'll keep cooler being all in one bag." asked Scruffy.

"Why not, less to carry," said Broozer.

"Yes sure," Chaffy agreed.

"Hand them over," shouted Scruffy. Broozer was the only one to throw his sandwiches over to Scruffy. Broozer always wore short trousers even in the winter, just to prove the point that he's tough even though goose pimples have been spotted on his legs in cold weather.

On the back of his hand, there is a self-made tattoo reading 'I Love Mum', which he is not proud of. He did it at the age of nine and was grounded for a month. He has black shoulder length hair, a stubbly nose, a nice smile, oh yes and rather large protruding ears, which he used to get teased about before he went to boxing lessons. But, now no body dares to tease him unless they want a punch in the nose.

"Hey, who has a new pair of trousers? Strut your stuff Prancer," shouted Broozer. Prancer always wore trousers under his kilt, he thought it looked cool.

"Let's have a ten minutes text session before we go," insisted Flyer MacHigher. She was the best skateboarder around. Her specialities are the 60 Ollie Heel flip, the Front foot impossible, and the Pop Shuvit. She also does a mental wheelie on her bike. Flyer has a very smiley face. She likes to keep her hair short, which is dark black and complements her light, bright brown eyes. Her grandma and grandad were born in India and are Sikhs. Her dad has the longest beard around for miles. She tends to spend far too long on her smartphone, so any excuse for text session, she'll be the suggester.

"Oooh," shouted Scruffy MacTuffy, "guess what? Jade has sent me a text."

"What does it say?" asked Broozer, as he rested his arm on Scruffy's shoulder.

"She said she is going to the pictures tomorrow night with Emma, fancy going?"

"Could do?" said Broozer, who had known Emma since they were babies. "But I'm not sure if I can afford it."

"Me either," sniffled Scruffy. Scruffy used to be Jade's best friend at pre-school before she moved out of the area to Liverpool, only coming back when her mum and dad visit friends.

All of the others were quiet texting. It was one of the best places in the area to get a text signal because there was a beacon just over the fence.

2. Bhreac Twins

"Come on, let's get going," suggested Prancer MacDancer. He thought of his name himself. He is probably one of the coolest in the gang. His mum lets him dye his hair sometimes with pink streaks. He is also the skinniest one out of all of them all and has the gangliest of all legs. He was called skinny banana legs at school. Normally on Saturdays, he would be at street dancing lessons. However, this Saturday, he just fancied hanging out with his gang. When the mood takes him, he shows off by doing dangerous stunts like running up walls then doing backward somersaults.

So, off they went zig-zagging down the road with Flyer showing off on her stunt bike doing a wheelie for about thirty metres. She had put some plastic square flaps tied on with pegs next to the wheels so that the spokes hit them to make her bike sound like a motorbike.

They arrived at the edge of the woods and got off their bikes at a special place where they hide their bikes under the branches of a huge fallen oak tree. Using all of their padlock cables, they tied their bikes together then wrapped the cable around a smaller tree branch.

As they fought their way through the woods, Scruffy continued to remind his mates about his dream being so real.

"It felt like I was being eaten alive. I could really feel it's slimy tonsils," Scruffy cried.

"I'm going in to catch the biggest fish you have ever seen today," boasted Chaffy, arriving at the river which runs into the Loch Ness.

Prancer said, "I'm going to catch a trout so we can cook it for supper."

There's trout in the river, but none of them has ever caught one, so today could be the lucky day.

"Let's go over the bridge further down the river this time, we may find the trout there," suggested Maltliquor MacSnigger as he combed his long black hair.

Maltliqour was very proud of his hair, sometimes his hair gets caught in his round bright orange glasses. He was slightly on the fat side because he was always drinking Coca-Cola. He was called Maltliquor MacSnigger because when he was younger, about three years ago, he ended up in hospital after drinking half a bottle of his dad's best whiskey when his mum and dad were holding a Christmas party. He sneaked downstairs and hid under the stairs with a friend who was having a sleep over. His friend also ended up in the hospital. That year he missed Father Christmas.

MacSnigger says, "He told the gang that he could see monsters and dragons dancing in front of his eyes for two days. Then it felt like the monsters and dragons were jumping up and down on his head for a week with the worst headache he had remembered." He also remembered chucking up for days.

They were all wearing black welly boots because it had been raining quite heavily except for Chaffy MacTaffy, who wore big black lace-up boots. He liked to wear brightly coloured clothes because his ginger curly hair matched with ginger freckles all over his face. He is the only one who was not born in Scotland. He was born in Wales and was very proud of it. He wore a green and white tartan and not red like the others. All of the others always know when he is nervous because he tends to stammer. He tries to control it through breathing exercises his mum had told him to do, but if he is really frightened, he forgets the breathing and just goes into a mega stammer.

They put all of their bags together in a heap under a small holly bush.

Chaffy MacTaffy said, "Let's spread out we'll have more of a chance to catch something, but first who has the maggots?"

"I've got them," shouted Maltliquor.

As he rummaged around in his bag, he accidentally knocked off the lid and all the maggots fell out spilling into his bag. He quickly grabbed his ham paste sandwiches and put them into another bag.

"Hurry up," shouted Broozer MacDoozer.

"Yes coming," shouted Maltliquor MacSnigger, not wanting anyone to know that he had spilled the maggots into his bag which had all the sandwiches. He nervously scooped the maggots up then he put them all back into the red plastic tub. Maltliquor tore up five squares pieces of tin foil, then put a handful of maggots on each piece and wrapped each one in turn.

"Here they are, come and get your maggots."

After collecting their maggots, they all moved further away from each other. Maltliquor MacSnigger shouted, "I'm going right around the corner near the weir I reckon that's where the trout are."

While Flyer sat on a piece of plastic next to Prancer and started texting friends. She wasn't too keen on fishing but liked hanging out with the boys. She had a soft spot for Prancer MacDancer, who she thought was cool. Flyer's eyes always lit up when he spoke to her.

Scruffy MacTuffy's fishing rod was longer than the rest of his friend's rods. He could get further under the trees on the other side of the river where the fish were, or so he thought.

"Hey, I've got a bite!" exclaimed Scruffy. "I told you there's fish under that tree."

He reeled it in without a struggle. It was a wee tiddler stickleback. He took it off his hook and threw it back into the river.

Chaffy MacTaffy suddenly shouted, "I've got one. And it's a big one."

"Do you want help?" Scruffy shouted.

"It's not a fish. It's something else." Chaffy shouted in a squeaky, shrilling voice, as he struggled to stop himself from being pulled into the river.

All the others came running over apart from Maltliquor MacSnigger, who was around the corner. Chaffy was having trouble reeling it in.

"What is it?" asked Flyer.

"I don't know," squeaked Chaffy.

"Wow, it could be a baby Loch Ness monster," joked Broozer.

They all stepped back a couple of steps with a "Woooow".

"My line is stuck. I just can't pull it at all," Chaffy said worriedly.

"Ooow, the line gone loose. I think it's playing with me now. WOW! Did you see that white tail come of the water?" As he pointed to the other side of the river. But nobody saw it.

"Reel it in, reel it in," shouted Scruffy.

"I can't," shouted Chaffy reclaiming his deep voice. He pulled and pulled, then the line went loose.

"Oh, I can reel it in now."

All the others stood back, expecting a big monster to land on the bank.

Chaffy shouted, "Are you ready?"

As he reeled in the last few feet, they all went "Awwwwh".

The line had snapped. There was nothing on the end.

"I reckon I caught a baby Loch ness Monster I know I did," said Chaffy MacTaffy.

"Don't be silly, Chaffy," said Flyer.

"Yer don't be silly. It was probably a pike or a big trout or even a rat," taunted Broozer.

"I don't know," said Chaffy, "I saw a tail."

"It was probably a piece of wood or weed," teased Flyer.

"Oh' well, let's get back to fishing," croaked Broozer, who was starting to get a cold and had a bit of a sore throat.

He didn't want to let the others know because he thought of himself a bit of a tufty. He had rare green eyes and blonde short straight hair, which he spiked up with hair gel.

Scruffy was daydreaming, trying to work out how he was going to get enough money to go the pictures.

"Hey, Broozer," said Scruffy, "are you going to the pictures tomorrow night? Because I don't think I have enough money."

"Not sure, I want to, it would be nice to see Emma, but I'm not sure where to get the money from."

"Me too," complained Scruffy, "maybe we could knock on a few doors asking if they want their cars washed. We only need to do six each, at £2 a pop."

"Yer maybe," Broozer said in an uninterested voice.

"Could you ask your da` Broozer? He's got plenty of money."

"Nar, I'm in 'is bad books because of not do'in me homework," answered Broozer.

Maltliquor MacSnigger didn't know anything about Chaffy MacTaffy's near catch because he had walked quite a way upstream. Maltliquor was having trouble with mosquitoes which kept buzzing around his ears and biting his neck. He was also feeling spooked and puzzled about noises in the woods behind him. He could hear branches cracking but could not see anything because it was really dark under the trees.

As he was pulling back a branch to have a look into the woods, out jumped the Hoot's twins. They gave him the fright of his life. He first thought it was a stag with antlers. Being a bit of a wimp, quickly he stepped back near the river not wanting to be spotted by the Hoot's twins. They were the local bullies. However, in his attempt to hide from the twins, he was out of view of all of his mates as well.

"O'y what you do'in 'ere?" said Bhreac Hoot with a nasty look on his face. "This is our river we live 'ere," he said while pushing Maltliquor.

"Yer wot you do'in 'ere?" Camdon Hoot said.

"I'm with my mates, and they're just around that bend," whimpered Maltliquor, pointing to further down the river.

Camdon said, "Give us yer fishing rod, come on give it and empty yer pockets and give us yer money."

Maltliquor wanted to shout to his mates, but thought that the twins would beat him up frightened him. So, he emptied his pockets of £2.41p, mainly in change.

"Where's yer phone? We want it," snarled Camdon.

"I don't have it, I left it with Flyer because her reception was bad," sniffled Maltliquor.

Bhreac Hoot suddenly grabbed his fishing rod and threw it into the deepest part of the river. As he threw it, the fishing reel caught Bhreac's jacket that was over his arm, both jacket and fishing rod sank slowly into the deep water.

"Now look what you 'ave made me do," said Bhreac. "Yer, my da is go'in to be really mad, and I'm go'in to tell 'im you threw my jacket in the river." After pushing Maltliquor even harder than the first time, making him fall over into the wet grass. The twins ran off.

Maltliquor went running back to his mates, waving his arms in the air. He was pretty upset that he had lost his favourite fishing rod and was wishing he had stayed closer to the gang. He told them all about what had happened and Chaffy told him about almost catching a baby Loch Ness monster.

3. Chunky Chews

They thought it might be the time to sit down and eat lunch and drink a can of Coca-Cola. They were hoping to have caught some trout because Prancer MacDancer had brought his dad's stove to cook them on. He always brings it when they go fishing just in case. They all took out their sandwiches and rolls. Flyer MacHigher said to Scruffy MacTuffy, "Why is it that you always get the best ham in your rolls when all of us get cheese or meat paste?"

"Arrrh, the trick is to always make your own," advised Scruffy. He took a large bite into his ham roll as he was very hungry. He was thinking how delicious it was. But as he was chewing something wiggled in his mouth. He quickly spat a mouthful of the half-chewed ham and bread on to the grass. There were three squidgy wrigley live maggots enjoying the remainder of his mouth full.

"Yuk, yuk, eeeer, how did they get in my roll?"

"Maybe you should get your mum to make your rolls in the future," joked Maltliquor.

Prancer was just about to take a bite out of his sandwich too, when a maggot creeped out between the two slices of bread, eyeballing him.

"Yuk," shouted Prancer, "how did that get in there?" They all looked inside their sandwiches and sure enough, all of them were crawling with squidgy diddley maggots, except for Chaffy, who had already eaten his sandwiches and had thought at the time that the ham paste tasted different. He had wondered why it had chewy lumpy bits in it.

"OW YUK no, no, I've eaten a maggot sandwich, YUK, but they are not alive in my tummy, I know it. I always chew my food really well," said Chuffy repulsed, as he spat onto the grass.

Maltliquor went quiet. "Hi guys, I have a confession," he said and started blushing. "I spilled the maggots into my bag. I thought I had scooped them all up, but some of them must have escaped into your sandwiches."

Prancer MacDancer said, "I'm hungry."

He picked six maggots out of his sandwich and flicked them into the river one at a time. Then he reassembled his sandwich and took a large bite.

"Mummy nice, just what the doctor ordered." Flyer, Broozer, and Maltliquor did the same and started to enjoy their sandwiches.

"Hey, they're only maggots," said Flyer.

"Oh yer, they all turn into blue bottles. Yuk, no way am I eating my sandwiches. You're welcome to eat them if you want," said Scruffy. He then added, "The thought of eating maggot's poo makes me want to gag."

"Maggot's poo, I didn't think of maggot's poo, and I have finished mine. Yuk, maggot's poo, I've eaten maggot's poo, yuk," complained Maltliquor, as he spat on the floor.

"I think we should look for a long stick so we can fish out Maltliquor's fishing rod," suggested Prancer, so off they went into the woods to find a long stick.

"This should do it. It's just the right length," shouted Broozer. They each had a go, but after about an hour of poking around in the river, they gave up.

"I think your fishing rod is lost forever," gasped Flyer.

"Yep, it's gone," Maltliquor sadly said.

"You can use my fishing rod," insisted Flyer, who was quite happy to get rid of it for the afternoon. She could now spend the time texting. The only trouble was that the signal was not a good one, so she had to keep moving about. They all put fresh maggots onto their hooks, which reminded Maltliquor of the maggot poo he had eaten. He began spitting again. Then they cast off their rods with a swish as far as they could, trying to get nearer the other side of the river.

"I've got a bite," cried Chaffy loudly.

"Not another Lock Ness monster," joked Scruffy with a smile.

"No," said Chaffy, "I think it's a big fish, but it feels different." His fishing rod was bent right over. It looked like it was going the snap in two. It was a struggle. At one point his line was going upriver then the opposite way downriver, reeling it in was quite hard.

"Here it comes wow, it's a big fat trout. Wow, wow, wow I'm the first to catch a trout," screamed Chaffy. It was so big that Chaffy could hardly get both hands around it. All of the others rushed over.

"Well done," said Scruffy.

"Who knows how to kill fish?" asked Broozer.

"I do," answered Chaffy but didn't want to pick up a slimy fish. So, he put on a brave face. Taking a deep breath as he took the hook out of its mouth, he swiftly bashed the fish over the head with a long heavy torch from his bag.

"That should do it. We can eat this one for supper later," bragged Chaffy, putting it into a plastic bag then into his bag.

"Who taught you how to kill fish?"

"My uncle goes fishing all of the time, he showed me," Chaffy said in a boastful voice.

The fish was right next to Maltliquor. Chaffy was just looking at it, thinking that ten minutes ago, it was swimming around in the river free and enjoying life, now it's dead. Suddenly it JUMPED into the air continued to flap around on the grass for a couple of seconds before becoming very still again. Maltliquor jumped with fright so far back that he tripped over a piece of wood just behind him and fell into the river. He couldn't swim, luckily the water was only a couple of inches deep near the edge.

He shouted, "THE FISH IS STILL ALIVE," as he crawled out of the river covered in mud. The others came over, while Prancer pulled Maltliquor to his feet.

Prancer explained, "Sometimes when fish are killed, they can still move, something to do with their nerves. It's certainly dead now," as he prodded it with a stick.

Scruffy MacTuffy suddenly shouted, "I've got one as well. It's a big 'an." As he reeled it in, the others watched in anticipation, surely enough it was so big it almost yanked his fishing rod out of his hand.

"It's another baby Loch Ness monster," sniggered Scruffy, as he reeled it in, they all stood back, especially Maltliquor MacSnigger. Scruffy reeled it in and pulled and pulled then out of the water popped the biggest fish they had ever seen.

"Wow, that's one big fish, I think it's a salmon," said Maltliquor.

"I hope I don't lose it," said Scruffy. It kept jumping high out of the water splashing back into the river. Prancer grabbed Scruffy's rod.

"I think with the two of us, we should be able to reel it in," said Prancer. After about half an hour, the fish must have got tired, but then so was Scruffy. When the line loosened, Scruffy was able to wind the fish in with the help of Prancer.

"Wow, we can eat this one," said Scruffy.

"Go on, Chaffy, do 'yer stuff. Bash it over the head," encouraged Broozer.

"Here you are Broozer, you have a go. You saw how I did it last time," teased Chaffy, not wanting to do it himself just in case it bit him.

"All right, give us your torch then," said Broozer.

Maltliquor quickly reached for the torch and gave it to Broozer, who quickly bashed it over the fish's head.

"There you go one dead fish, I've killed it. So, who is going to gut it?"

They all stepped back as Flyer stepped forward and said, "I will," to the surprise of the boys. She quickly gutted it just like her mum had shown her and the boys watched, all pulling faces of disgust.

"Yuk," said Broozer.

4. The Bite

Flyer then went down to the river to give it a good wash. She held it by the tail. It was heavy, so half of the fish was in the water.

Brrr, Brrr, Brrr her phone started to ring. She reached into her pocket for the phone leaving one hand to hold the fish. Being so heavy it lowered further into the water, suddenly there was a stir in the water with a large splash, and the fish was gone. Flyer was left holding the tail.

"EEEEEEEEEEK," she screamed.

The boys came running over. Flyer was standing looking quite pale, holding only a fishtail attached to about a sixteenth of a fish in the shape of a huge bite.

"Oh, where's are fish?" shouted Prancer MacDancer.

"Let's get out of here before what ate the fish eats us," screeched Maltliquor.

Scruffy grabbed his bag, and the first fish they had caught, which looked a bit of a tiddler compared to the fish that had just been eaten. All the others grabbed their bags putting them over their shoulders, then they headed back through the woods. The Six Macs tied their fishing rods to their bikes then off they went with speed.

"The first one to camp, cooks the fish," shouted Broozer, who was second one-off followed by the rest.

"I think that is going to be Maltliquor," said Scruffy. He knew that Maltliquor only had to put a bag over his shoulder and had left in speed a few minutes earlier.

Surely enough, Maltliquor MacSnigger was first back quickly followed by Prancer, Flyer, Scruffy, Chaffy, and Broozer. As soon as they got off their bikes, they all got out their smartphones and started texting all of their friends telling them what had happened, that lasted for about twenty minutes.

"Who's got the fish?" asked Prancer.

"I have," answered Scruffy, "Maltliquor is cooking it."

"Am I?" answered Maltliquor in surprise.

"Yes, you are first back," snapped Broozer.

"OK, I'll do it, my mum said I am really good at cooking fish," smirked Maltliquor, not wanting to pick up the slimy fish.

Scruffy took out the trout from Chaffy's bag, then unwrapped it from the plastic bag and placed it onto the grass. It looked so small compared to the huge salmon.

"Let's light a fire instead of using Prancer's dad's stove. It's more fun," suggested Flyer, who liked warm fires.

"Who's got the matches?" asked Chaffy.

"Here you are," answered Scruffy, as he threw them over to Chaffy.

The fire lit quickly inside an old metal water tank full of dry wood and embers from previous fires. The water tank was from the old tip just over the fence. Since most of their camp was littered with bits and pieces, they were always adding things.

They even had a kitchen sink with a tap that was connected to a water tank that was high up in the tree so it can catch rainwater. The water was used to make cups of tea.

Just so he didn't have to pick up the fish, Maltliquor put a stick into the trout's mouth and scooped it up. He placed it inside the metal tank on top of the fire. The trout cooked quickly burning on the outside, which Maltliquor was teased about later. Being so small they all had only about one mouthful each which was hardly worth the fishes' life.

"I'm still hungry," groaned Prancer, "it's almost supper time I think we should go home and meet back here really early at seven o'clock tomorrow morning."

"We should take our fishing rods with us again I want to catch another salmon, but I must be back at home by two o'clock, so that I have enough time to earn some money from washing cars," insisted Scruffy, while thinking of supper and food, food, food, and more food.

"We should bring packed lunches again. We don't want to get hungry, do we? All agree?" asked Maltliquor.

They all agreed.

"In the morning, we could look for something in the old tip with a hook on, so that we can get Maltliquor MacSnigger's fishing rod out the river," suggested Flyer.

"Good idea," Scruffy agreed.

They gathered around in a circle then held up their arms and touched fists and shouted, "The Six Mac's." Then jumped on their bikes and rode home as fast as they could. When scruffy MacTuffy got home, he looked at his smart phone and saw that Jade had texted him.

It read, "R U coming 2 morrow?"

He thought for a while, then texted back, "Yes, see you outside the Odean at six. We could grab a burger first."

Jade's text then read: "C U tomorrow."

Scruffy thought some more, "Hmmm, how am I going to get the money?"

He texted Broozer, "Just texted Jade and said I'm going to meet her at six but I still don't have any money, are you coming?"

"You are mad, I don't have any money," Broozer texted back, "We can wash cars after we've got Maltliquor's rod," texted Scruffy.

"OK, let's do it, see you tomorrow," texted Broozer.

5. The Fall

The next morning, all of them were up early. They more or less arrived at their camp at the same time. They started with their ritual, by forming a circle all facing inwards shoulder to shoulder then arms stretched into the air, they touched hands with clenched fists and shouted, "THE SIX MACS." They had a ten-minute text session afterwards.

"My da said it was probably a large pike that took a bite out of the fish," Flyer told the group.

"Yer' it probably was," Broozer agreed.

"No, it was something else I saw a tail and it was white. Pikes aren't white they are brown," said Chaffy.

"Hey Maltliquor, what have you got in your bag? It looks like you are moving a house?" joked Broozer, knowing that his bag was full of Coca-Cola cans.

"There's not much. There are just a few sandwiches and a couple of cans of drink," answered Maltliquor protectively.

"Right, let's go and look for something long with a hook on the end so that we can fish out Maltliquor fishing rod," suggested Broozer, thinking that the quicker they retrieve the fishing rod, the quicker he and Scruffy could start washing cars.

"What about this?" asked Chaffy, pointing to an old curtain rod.

"No, that's wee too short," sneered Scruffy.

After about thirty minutes of looking, nothing could be found. Maltliquor was getting despondent.

Then Prancer shouted, "What about this?" picking up a long pole with a hook on the end. "I think it pulled shop blinds down. My granddad used to have one for his wet fish shop."

"How will we get it on our bikes?" asked Flyer.

"We can use two bikes, one at the front and one at the back," answered Prancer.

"Let's hope we don't get stopped by the police," said Chaffy nervously.

"It looks dangerous to me. I think we should strap the pole to our bikes then walk," argued Maltliquor.

"Where is your sense of adventure Maltliquor?" jeered Prancer, who volunteered straight away, and took one end.

Flyer grabbed the other end. They are the two daredevils, especially Prancer, who likes a good challenge. He was the tallest one out of the six, so his bike was almost an adult's one.

They put their bags of sandwiches and drinks over their heads then off they went. Prancer and Flyer looked a bit wobbly on their bikes. Still the plan seemed to be working apart from strange looks from people in passing cars. One car hooted, as it passed Prancer went wobbly, so wobbly that he lost concentration and wobbled straight into the hedge, falling off his bike straight into a pile of stinging nettles. Flyer followed fast landing on top of Prancer, which broke her fall.

"Ow, Ow OWWWW," cried Prancer. He was jumping up and rolling Flyer into the stinging nettles as well.

"Ow, ow ow, ooooow," cried Flyer. Both stood together, rubbing their arms and legs. Prancer went in head-first and almost immediately started getting lumps all over his nose. The stinging nettles stung him right up to his underpants under his kilt because that morning he had decided not to wear trousers under his kilt.

"It's sensitive up there, one more inch, and the nettles would have stung my willy," joked Prancer.

All the other were laughing, Maltliquor was laughing so much he nearly wet his shorts.

"Come on! Back on your bikes," said Chaffy.

"Your turn now," shouted Prancer, who was still rubbing his legs. Broozer grabbed one end of the pole, and Scruffy grabbed the other end, and off they went again. The woods were just around the corner.

On arriving, there were loads of trucks, lorries, and diggers with lots of people dressed in orange vis jackets. A lady approached Flyer, and said, "You can't come down here. We are dredging the river, it's CLEAN up time." They all looked at each other. Broozer thought, 'Great we can go back home.'

Scruffy said to the others, "I know a way through the woods that will take us straight to where Maltliquor's rod was."

They took the pole off their bikes, then placed their bikes carefully under the oak tree, padlocking them all together.

"Bring the pole," shouted Prancer, who was still rubbing his legs and arms. He was also feeling a bit worried about the lumps on his nose, which were tingling.

"How are your legs, Flyer?" asked Prancer.

"Not too bad just a bit itchy," Flyer replied.

"OOOOH, my nose doesn't feel very nice at all," grumbled Prancer.

"Oww, it looks all lumpy. It needs some cream on it," replies Flyer.

It took three of them to carry the long pole through the woods. Maltliquor expressed concern that he felt that they were being watched. He was having that eerie feeling that makes your hair stand up on the back of your neck. They arrived at the spot were Maltliquor's fishing rod was thrown in.

"Stick the pole in here," suggested Chaffy.

They fished around with the pole, which was rather heavy, for a whole hour. But without any luck what so ever. The river was just too deep.

A man approached them and asked, "What are you doing lads?" Maltliquor told him the story.

"Well lads, you are in for a bit of luck. We are draining one mile of the river. It will all be done in five hours, then tomorrow we are going to clean the bed of old rusty bikes and prams. You will be able to get your fishing rod then."

"I can't believe why people throw rubbish into river like old trollies and bikes, it must poison all types of river life," sighed Flyer.

"Oh yes, all rivers are totally polluted with old rusty bikes, drink cans, trollies, prams, and lots of other things. We should get a whole lorry load tomorrow," said the man.

"That's sad," Prancer said as he bowed his head.

Broozer and Scruffy both looked at each other, then at their phones.

"Five hours, it's eight o'clock now, that takes us to one o'clock then back to camp, then home, nobody likes their cars cleaned in the afternoon. Most adults prefer their cars cleaned in the morning so we may not get enough money for tonight. How can we get out of this one?" complained Scruffy.

"We have to help each other it's in our rules, we are 'The Six Macs'," stressed Broozer.

"'Yer, I suppose we do have to help Maltliquor get his fishing rod today. It's our only chance, tomorrow the river will be full again, so maybe we can't go tonight," sniffled Scruffy, who never carried any tissue paper about with him so that he can blow his nose.

6. The Bridge

"We have five hours to kill before we can get Maltliquor MacSnigger's fishing rod. Why don't we go into the wood on the other side of the river, and see if we can find any snakes? There must be some in there," suggested Broozer MacDoozer, who liked catching anything that moved then keeping them as pets.

"We haven't been in there before. I think there's quite a steep hill that looks over the loch with loads of climbable rocks," explained Prancer.

"How do you know if you have never been in there before?" sneered Scruffy.

"Arh, I said we haven't been in there, but I have. I went there with my dad about a year ago. He likes to watch birds and there's a good view at the top right over the loch," Prancer explained, still rubbing his groin trying not to let the others see while thinking quietly about of his good looks spoilt by a lumpy tingling red nose.

"There's another bridge further up the river. We can cross over there," pointed Prancer.

So off they went, Prancer started showing off by climbing up a tree then doing a couple of somersaults, but he landed badly with a BUMP. Suddenly feeling really embarrassed, he hid his face under his hoodie. He felt his face going the same colour as his nose.

"That 'er teach 'yer," laughed Scruffy.

Prancer scooped himself off the ground brushing the mud off his kilt, then pushing past his mates as he wanted to get to the front of the group because he knew where the bridge was.

"Cor doesn't Prancer look like Rudolf the Red Nose Reindeer with added bumpy bits," joked Scruffy.

"No, he looks like Prancer the red-nosed reindeer," chuckled Broozer.

Prancer went quiet as he didn't like being teased. They arrived at the bridge, but it couldn't really be called a bridge. There were loads of holes in it and the wood was rotten with lots of wormholes. It had cheesy bobs and worms crawling all over, making a very wet slippery surface. It looked like if you stood on it, it would entirely collapse into the river which was rather deep. Maltliquor was the first one to say something.

"I'm not going across that," he complained.

"Me either," said Chaffy. Prancer walked back quietly away from the bridge. He grabbed the long pole with the hook, then started to run really fast towards the bridge, but he had to drop the pole as it was too heavy to carry. He ran right over to the other side jumping over all of the holes.

"That's how it's done," he shouted.

Then Flyer did the same, followed by Broozer and Scruffy, who brought over the pole. They then stuffed it under a bush out of sight. All four were over the other side jumping up and down, and waving their arms shouting, "Jump, Jump, Jump, Jump, Jump." Chaffy Mactaffy and Maltliquor MacSnigger found them a bit intimidating.

"Come on," shouted Prancer.

"'Yer come on! Jump!" jeered Broozer.

Chaffy looked at the bridge then thought, 'Oh just go for it,' then he took a deep breath and ran as fast as he could across the bridge. He was over about three-quarters of the way when there was a loud creak, a large piece of wood from the bridge fell into the water with a PLOP. Being so rotten it sank for a while then slowly came up to the surface before floated downstream.

Chaffy got a fright. He ran a little faster. Then he finished off by jumping into mid-air before landing on the long damp grass on the other side.

"Phew, mmmade it," he said in a shaky voice. The bridge was still intact, but now there was just a slightly larger hole in it, looking even more menacing.

"Come on Maltliquor," shouted the others.

"Jump, Jump, Jump, Jump, Jump," they taunted.

Maltliquor went up to the bridge and looked at it, and thought, *'No, I can't. What if I fall in? I can't swim, no, no, I can't.'*

"Jump, jump, jump! Come on! We are here for your fishing rod," the others shouted.

"I can't. I may fall in, or the bridge might collapse," Maltliquor squeaked.

"Come on! Don't be a wimp, you're holding us up," shouted Chaffy.

He was over the other side, safe and feeling smug. Maltliquor decided he will go for it. Instead of running for it, he slowly started to cross the bridge one foot at a time grabbing tightly to the handrail. He was nervously stepping over the holes as the bridge creaked and moaned. SUDDENLY he slipped.

"AHHHH." Falling sideways one leg slid down a hole, which dangled in the water. Prancer ran to the middle grabbing his arms then pulling him, so his leg was out of the water.

"Quick grab my other arm Maltliquor," insisted Prancer. Maltliquor went to grab his arm, but because he was so scared of falling into the river and maybe drowning, he missed. Then he fell backward onto the creaky bridge. Prancer just grabbed his legs and pulled him along the slippery surface to the other side on to the grass verge.

"You don't call me Prancer MacDancer for nothing," he proudly said. Shaken, Maltliquor wasn't too happy.

His butt was now all wet and his trousers were green and slightly slimy. He flipped the ring pull of a can of coke then started gulping it down finishing the lot in seconds.

"How many cans do have in your bag?" asked Flyer.

"Not many, just a few," answered Maltliquor. Not wanting to reveal how many he had just in case one of them might start to tease him by saying, "You've got too many I think you should give us one."

Prancer clenched his fist then put his arm in the air. All the others did the same then they touched fist and shouted, "The Six Macs."

"You see, we would have never let any harm come to you. We are the Macs and we help each other, AGREED," ranted Prancer.

They all shouted, "**YEEEEER**, THE SIX MACS."

Then off they went into the woods, lifting up every piece of wood looking for grass snakes, slow worms, toads and mice.

"Don't you feel as if you're being watched? It's a bit spooky in this wood." Maltliquor gulped.

"I know what you mean. It's quite eerie," agreed Broozer They started to climb up a steep hill which had bracken dotted in-between green algae-covered boulders. The boulders scratched Chaffy's legs being the only one not wearing welly boots. Prancer was in his element darting in between rocks and jumping up the hill faster than the rest.

"I wish I had brought my mountain bike, I could have had so much fun," cried Flyer.

7. Spooky Cave

"Next time, we could come back next weekend. We can all bring our bikes. It will be fun," shouted Prancer, as he disappeared over a boulder. Just before the top, they came across a large opening in the side of the hill.

"Ooow, what's this?" howled Scruffy, as he put his head inside a cave.

"A caaave, ooow let's go in," insisted Broozer.

"Is it safe?" inquired Maltliquor.

"You worry too much Maltliquor," said Flyer.

"It's not my fault it's my mum's. She's worried about everything. I think I take after her," said Maltliquor.

They started walking down a steep hill down into the cave.

"BOOOOOO," Scruffy jumped out in front of Maltliquor, and Maltliquor jumped into the air and nearly bumped his head on the cave ceiling.

"That's not funny," he yelled.

"Only having some fun," joked Scruffy.

The cave started to get dark. It smelled damp and musty. The floor was wet and slightly slippery. They all switched on the lights of their mobile phones, which were rather dim.

"I think we should come back next week with proper torches. It's too dark to see if there are any holes and it's spooky," fretted Maltliquor.

They all agreed and turned around, just as they turned they heard a roaring noise which echoed through the cave. It made them all run out of the cave as fast as they could. When they got out they all fell to the ground with exhaustion after running up the steep hill.

"Wwwow, dddid you hear that? Now, that wasn't a large ppppike or a big rrrrat," stammered Chaffy. They carried on climbing to the top hill till they reached the top. What a view there was, with not a single cloud in the sky. It reflected blue on to the still loch. There were birds flying in groups across the water with swans bobbing around with their cygnets.

"I can see why your dad comes up here Prancer. It's one of those places that you can really explore," remarked Flyer, wanting to take off her top because she was so hot but felt self-conscious in front of the boys.

They sat there for a while, enjoying the warm sun on their faces. "I'm bored we still have three and a half hours to kill," groaned Flyer.

Prancer suggested that he run back down the hill to get their bike torches. He was the only one who was fearless about going over the bridge so that they could explore the cave.

"Great idea. We'll meet you at the cave's entrance," suggested Broozer.

So, off went Prancer MacDancer. He had disappeared before anyone could say another word. All of the others got out their smart phones for a text session.

"Awww, there's no signal here. What about yours Flyer?" moaned Chaffy.

"Me too," sighed Flyer, as she started climbing a tree and then began dangling upside-down by her legs. The boys decided to have a rough and tumble, started by Broozer. He grabbed Scruffy around the neck and rolled him to the ground.

"Hey Broozer! Ooow! You can be too rough sometimes," objected Scruffy.

Chaffy then jumped on to Broozer.

"Owww, ow, I've got a rock under my back, get off me Chaffy, Owww that hurt," shouted Broozer, as he got up rubbing his back.

Broozer thought he would join Flyer up the tree.

Someone's smart phone went beep, beep. It was Scruffy's, which was odd seeing they couldn't get a signal.

It read, "We have made a mistake the film we want to c is tomorrow night, and mum and dad have decided to stay until Tuesday so we will meet u 2 morrow night at 5 if that is OK?" "Great," shouted Scruffy.

Then he told Broozer, who said, "That takes the pressure off and gives us another day to find the money."

"I will have to ask my dad if I can go," said Scruffy.

Meanwhile, Prancer had ran over the bridge, and through the wood, arriving back by the bikes. He quickly took off all the lights and put them into his bag. He went running back when arriving at the bridge he noticed that most of the water had been drained out of the river and it looked only about two feet deep. As he ran over the bridge, quite a few pieces of wood fell into the river. In fact, he thought while crossing it that it felt like it was going to collapse, but it didn't matter because they would be able to walk across the river bed on the way back.

He then started running back up the hill towards the cave but slowed down to a walk because his legs were starting to feel tired. Wondering where Prancer was? The others were now hovering around the entrance of the cave. He had been away for quite a while. Scruffy's head was still sore from the bump the day before, which reminded him of his scary dream he had that morning. He then started to tell the rest of them about it again.

"Not again, Scruffy. We've heard it a million times," complained Chaffy. He then decided to go into the cave by himself just a short way in, leaving the others at the entrance. Suddenly out of the dark, a big pair of green eyes appeared. Scruffy froze with fear and before he could run or even shout a great big head knocked him over, then all he could see was a big open mouth coming towards him.

Before he knew it, he was in the monster's mouth just like his dream, which was slimy with the stinkiest of all smells.

"HELP, HELP, HEEEEEELP," squeaked Scruffy like a mouse being eaten by a cat.

The monster quickly took him right into the deepest part of the dark cave where he was dropped into a cold, shallow pool of twigs and slime. He quickly stood up and wanted to run, but there was so much green slime he could not get his feet off the bottom of the muddy pool. There was the smelliest of all smells like stale fish. There were two baby monsters with big green eyes looking down on him. He could see them because there was an opening in the top of the cave and the sun was shining through.

All he could think of was that, he might be eaten alive just like his dream. He IS lunch. He was so scared, but he didn't want to make any noise as it may attract more attention to him. He was just about to cry for help when one of the smaller monsters flipped its tail, hitting Scruffy behind his knees knocking him into the slime. Since he had his mouth open, he got a mouth full of the green slimy, smelly stuff.

Instantly he spat it out.

"YUK, BLUULUUR, YUK, BLUUUUUULEER, that tasted like smelly fish."

He managed to slither himself on to the side away from the baby monsters. He was quite surprised that he has not been eaten. Then he noticed halfway up one of their tails was a fishing hook attached to a fishing float connected to a stretch of fishing line.

'**Arrrhh**, so Chaffy did catch a baby Loch Ness monster,' he thought. He saw a small hole in the side of the cave wall and was able to climb inside it. There was no sign of the dad Loch Ness monster, so he felt safe for now. He thought if he shouts for help every five minutes, the gang would find him eventually.

"HELP, HELP I'M DOWN HERE." But then he thought if they find him, they may get eaten, maybe he should try to escape by himself.

"Shush! did you hear Scruff's voice shouting help?" whispered Chaffy.

"No, I didn't hear anything he's probably been eaten by the Loch Ness monster," joked Broozer.

"SCRUFFY, Scruffy," shouted Flyer.

"Scruffy, stop joking around, come out, come on, stop joking Scruffy," shouted Maltliquor. They all went a little way into the cave very cautiously.

"SCRUFFY, Scruffy, SCRUFFY," they all shouted, but there was not a sound. You could hear a pin drop. **"BOOOOOOO!"** shouted Prancer, really loud. They all jumped.

"That's not funny," snapped Maltliquor.

"Scruffy has disappeared. He's not here, anywhere," said Chaffy.

"His dream has probably come true. He's been eaten by the Loch Ness monster," joked Prancer.

"Ha, Ha," they all laughed except Maltliquor MacSnigger. He expressed concern, "Maybe he has been eaten, if he has, you'll all be sorry."

"Dddon't be silly Maltliquor. He's **pppprobably** hiding, come out Scruffy, a joke 's a joke, **ccccome** on come out, ddddon't be silly you are making Maltliquor **nnervous**. In fact, you're making us all **nnnervous, ccome out, ccccome** out Scruffy," stammered Chaffy.

Still, there was no noise and no Scruffy. They put on all of their torches. The cave had a lot of stalactites hanging from the ceiling which were dripping cold water on to their head. There were a few stalagmites growing out from the ground which could be quite dangerous if one of them slipped and fell on to one. The ground was quite slippery with green slimy plants growing up the walls. It was also very cold, and because they all had short-sleeved shirts on, it felt even colder.

Prancer noticed the cold soothed his legs from the stinging nettle stings and his nose was less red if he looked boss-eyed at it. But there was no sign of Scruffy.

"Scruffy, Scruffy," they shouted.

"I'm hungry, can we sit down and eat our sandwiches?" blurted Maltliquor, who was at the back of the group.

"How can you even think about eating knowing that Scruffy may have been eaten, or he may have fallen down a hole or anything, or we may never see him again?" sniffled Flyer. In fact, they were all starting to sniffle because their noses were really cold.

8. The Rescue

Suddenly, they all heard a huge roar which came from deep inside the dark cave.

They all stopped.

"What was that?" shuddered Maltliquor.

"I don't know, but I think it may be something to do with Scruffy's disappearance. We have to go in further to find him," quivered Broozer, who is normally the brave one.

"But it may have eaten him, and it might eat us," shivered Maltliquor.

"My dad said, "that if the Loch Ness monster does exist, it probably only eats fish, or it is more like a duck. Eating snails, grass, algae, aquatic plants, and roots," so it won't eat us because we are meat," stated Chaffy.

"STOP," shouted Prancer who was at the front. He shone his torch on the ground there was a large hole which was one and a half metres wide with a long drop.

"We can jump it," bragged Prancer. He took a few steps back and took a huge jump leaping over to the other side. He didn't quite make it, slipping backwards then twisting in mid-air quickly grabbing the edge pulling then himself up.

"PHEW that was lucky, I nearly had my lot," he wailed, sitting on the cold, wet floor thinking to himself how he was going to get back across. All the other looked into the hole. "I'm not jumping that," whimpered Maltliquor nervously. "Well, I think nnnnone of us should jjjjump. It's far too dddddangerous," stammered Chaffy.

"All of you go outside and look for a plank long enough to place over the hole, I'll stay here," Prancer told them. "You've got to stay here, woo-hooo don't get eaten," joked Flyer.

At that point, there was another loud roar, "ROAR." It seemed to be louder and nearer than before. So Prancer wasn't too keen on being left on his own. They all wormed their way out of the cave slowly. When they got out, the sun was so bright that they all squinted and couldn't see anything for about five minutes, but it was nice to feel the warm sun on their faces. Once they could see, Broozer said, "Let's split up and meet back in fifteen minutes."

So off they went, after about five minutes Broozer came across a VW van boot door with no glass in it, but it was too heavy for him to lift. He thought it would be ideal, so he went back to the cave and waited another five minutes for the rest to come back. Chaffy had pulled back a large long piece of tree, but it wasn't very heavy and looked rotten with wormholes. The other two had nothing.

"I've found the perfect bridge. It's the door of a van, but it's heavy and will need all of us to carry it," Broozer MacDoozer told them. They arrived at the door. All took a corner and carried it back to the cave.

"Take your belt off Broozer so that we can strap the torches on to the door," asked Chaffy.

"I think my trousers will fall down without my belt I'll use my scarf," said Broozer.

They managed to strap two of the torches to the door. Then they started to walk carefully into the cave. It was unpredictably precarious because the torches only shone straight ahead, so they couldn't see the ground. After a while, they reached the hole, but there was no sign of Prancer. "Prancer, where are you?" shouted Flyer. A rather pale looking Prancer appeared from behind a rock.

"What's wrong?" asked Broozer.

"I thought you were the monster. My eyes adjusted to the dark very quickly so I saw it. I saw the Loch Ness monster. It's huge, and it looks angry. I'm sure it was looking for me. It kept sniffing really loudly. I hid over there in that corner and it stinks, poooooo. It stinks like rotten fish, but worse," complained Prancer in a babbled voice. "What have you there?" he shouted.

"It's a VW boot door I think it will just fit over the hole. The only trouble with it is that there's a big hole where glass was and on one side of the door there are jagged, sharp pieces of metal sticking up," Broozer cautiously said.

"So, we will have to use the opposite side, but we will have to watch out that we don't trip up on the door handle," advised Flyer.

They lifted up on to its end then dropped it over the hole, it only just fitted, but being a door, it was really strong. Chaffy and Broozer held a corner each, and Prancer held the door on his side. Flyer was first, she hardly touched it, just one foot in the middle, a jump, then over. Once over, she was able to hold one of the corners.

"Go on. Maltliquor we are all holding a corner each it's safe," assured Broozer. Maltliquor hesitated then with one foot in the middle jumped over. Broozer went next. When it was Chaffy's turn, they could only hold one end of the door. As he jumped one of his shoelaces caught the boot handle tripping him over and dragging the VW boot door over the edge. Before he could shout for help, the VW boot door crashed down the hole with Chaffy following. His scarf caught on a piece of jagged rock which stopped him crashing to the bottom. The door was so heavy that it pulled off his boot, where it should have pulled off his leg. Instead of the VW door crashing to the bottom, it got stuck halfway down.

"HHHHELP,   HHHELP,"   shouted   Chaffy. Immediately Prancer tied all off their scarves together, tying one end to a stalagmite. He then lowered himself down the hole.

"Can you grab my feet Chaffy?" asked Prancer.

"Yyyes, I can jjjjjjust rrrrrreach," stammered Chaffy. He grabbed one of Prancer's wellies. The others then started pulling them both up by pulling the scarf.

"Something strange is happening. I'm slipping down. What's happening?" Chaffy shouted. Prancer realised that his welly boot was slipping off.

"Quick, quick pull us up by my welly boot. Its slipping off, Chaffy could die, quick, quick pull, pull," shouted Prancer to the others.

They all pulled as fast as they could. Prancer grabbed Broozer's hand, who then pulled him onto the cave floor with his legs still over the edge. Flyer lent over the hole stretching down, grabbing Prancer's welly boot to save Chaffy from falling. The boot was almost off his foot when suddenly Maltliquor reached down even further grabbing Chaffy's shirt and pulled him up to safety.

"Cor blimey! That was a bit brave for you, Maltliquor. You and Prancer are the heroes of the day," complemented Flyer.

"Well, if I hadn't grabbed him, he would have lost Prancer's welly boot," Maltliquor joked.

"That was a close call we have to be more careful. The only trouble is that we are now stuck this side in-between a deep hole and a monster, who could eat us.

Whose idea was it to come into this cave?" quivered Maltliquor, as he opened another can of coke.

"Yyyou cccdould have stayed at the opening and not **ccccome** with us. It's your cccchoice you hhhere," stammered Chaffy. Cautiously, they started the descent down a steep path inside the cave, shinning their torches everywhere. All of them were very quiet.

"Dddid you hear Ssscruffy's vvvvoice?" squeaked Chaffy, who's voice had reverted back from a deep voice to voice that now sounded more like of a small boy.

"Yes, I heard it," cried Flyer.

"ROOOOOR."

"Ooow that was a lot nearer than Scruffy's shout," shivered Maltliquor MacSnigger.

"We have to be brave we are the Six Macs, fists up!" cheered Prancer. Shouting very loud, five of them touched fists.

"The Six Macs," which wasn't a very good idea because there was another loud, "ROOOOOOR," which was even nearer.

"Over there are loads of stalagmites, we can hide behind them," advised Flyer. So they all carefully climbed over a load of wobbly rocks trying not to trip or slip over them. Then they wriggled through the stalagmites until they had got through about eleven of them. All five of them then crouched down onto the wet slimy cave floor.

"Here we are, let's put this dark green raincoat over us all. It will give up some camouflage," suggested Flyer.

"Torches off," whispered Chaffy. They all switched their torches off. The cave went totally black. It was cold and very spooky.

"It may smell us out," boomed Maltliquor.

"Shut up, it will hear us," whispered Flyer.

"Rooooar, Rooooar, ROOOAR."

The cave floor started to rummble.

"Ooooow, there's **sssomething really bbbig ccccoming,"** stammered Chaffy quietly. They felt the presence of something very big, that stopped right next to the stalagmites where the five macs were hiding.

"Why has it stopped?" whispered Maltliquor, in a hushed voice.

"Shhhhhh, shut up," whispered Broozer, putting his finger up to his mouth, which no one could see.

"Roooooooar." There was something in the dark making sniffing noises. The five Macs could feel a warmness in the air from the monster's hot body, but could not see anything at all. They were frozen with fear. Their eyes slowly started adjusting to the darkness after switching their torches off. They started to see a shady outline of a huge monster with a slender long neck and a smallish head moving towards them. It moved so close to them that all they could see was one large foot, then they could feel something very close just above the raincoat snorting and sniffing. All five stayed very still. Then with a great big snort which almost blew off the raincoat, it suddenly lifted its head and went away.

They could hear the monster's footsteps slowly getting softer away from them. The cave then went quiet with an eerie stillness.

"BOOOOO," shouted Broozer.

They all jumped out of the skins.

"Oh, very funny, ha, ha. Do you really want the monster to come back?" complained Chaffy, as they all put their torches back on.

Flyer shouted, "Yuk! Look at my raincoat. It's covered in slime and pooooo. Smell that,"

They all smelt Flyer's coat.

"POOOOOOO what a smell of smelly fish my coat is ruined," Flyer cried, as she rolled it up inside-out before putting it into her bag.

"Look on the bright side, thanks to your coat we weren't eaten, and the monster has gone," Broozer said, thankfully. "For now, but we're not out of the woods, yet. There's only one way back and there's a large hole in the way," expressed Chaffy.

"No, out of the stalagmites." interrupted Maltliquor.

Chaffy continued, "Ha, yer' very funny, but we have to get a move on its twelve o'clock in the afternoon. We have only six hours to find Scruffy. My mum and dad will give me real grief if I'm not home in time for supper.

In fact, I will be grounded for a week after being late last weekend."

"Yer me too, my mum's last words were 'Don't be late'," added Prancer.

"Me too, I have to be back by seven," stated Flyer.

"Well, we better get moving and rescue Scruffy, come on, let's run for it," insisted Prancer. Off they went trying to run down the cave without slipping over. Maltliquor was becoming anxious because he didn't like dark caves. He only had eight cans of Coca-Cola left. He also was starting to get a toothache from a bad tooth he has had for a while, and had been waiting to have it removed. They could hear Scruffy's shouting for help getting nearer. Broozer's torch started to go very dim.

"Hey Broozer, your torch is running out of battery," said Flyer.

"Yer' I know I keep meaning to ask dad to buy new ones. Let's hope all of your batteries are OK or we'll be in the dark and never get out here, and probably all be eaten alive. That's why we have to get out of here as soon as possible after rescuing Scruffy," said Broozer gallantly. The cave started to get bigger. Then in front of them, to their surprise were two baby Loch Ness monsters, who were about two metres high.

They heard Scruffy's nervous voice coming from a corner of the cave. "SCRUFFY," shouted Chaffy.

"I'm here, I'm stuck here. The baby monsters are blocking my way and they look mean," sniffled scared

Scruffy, who was rather cold from being in the same spot for quite a while. Flyer went over to them, "They look harmless to me," she said. As she touched one of their tales, it didn't turn around to bite her. It just pulled its tail away then continued eating slimy green Loch weed.

"There you go. They are plant eaters they don't eat meat. They're friendly," said Flyer, while she touched one of the plant eaters again.

"Or is it because they don't have any teeth yet?" asked Maltliquor.

9. The Chase

"Come out, Scruffy they are friendly," assured Flyer. They all got out their smart phones and started to take photos and selfies with the monsters in the background. Broozer who liked keeping snakes spotted something under all of the green smelly slime. It was a monster's egg. It was the same colour as the slime, so the others had missed seeing it. He knew that if he said let's take one the other would say certainly no, so he sneakily put one of them into his bag which fitted perfectly.

"Dad is going to be so proud of me. We are the first to discover the Loch Ness monster. We are going to be famous," stated Chaffy, who was now feeling less nervous.

Maltliquor suddenly shrieked, "Nobody answered my question, what if these babies are friendly because they don't have any teeth yet? What if the big monster has really sharp teeth and eats young boys and girls just for fun? The other question is if that's the mum monster where's dad? So I think we should get out of here before the monster comes back."

"Don't worry, Maltliquor, we'll get out of here, we are 'The Six Macs'," answered Flyer.

"But first, we have to take Chaffy's fishing hook out of that baby monsters' tail," suggested Scruffy.

"So, I did catch a baby Loch Ness monster yesterday," cheered Chaffy Mactaffy.

"I don't think it counts as a catch, you caught its tail. It didn't bite your maggot," taunted Broozer.

"I still think it counts as a catch," stated Prancer.

"So, who's brave enough to take the hook out?" asked Flyer.

"I'll do it," said Broozer if two of you hold it down. Chaffy and Scruffy grabbed the tail then held it down, both slipping into the smelly slime.

"PPPPPooooo, pooo, pppoooo, yuk that sssmells," stammered Chaffy. Broozer carefully removed the hook, he took some antiseptic cream out of his bag which his mum had given him. He smoothed the cream on to the wound, then he wrapped his tartan red scarf around its tail which he wasn't too happy with. "There you go, that should do it. It will be better in no time," he proudly said.

"Can I have some of that cream for my nose?" asked Prancer.

"Sure, here you go. I should have remembered I had it earlier it would have soothed your nose," apologised Broozer.

"I think we should get out of here, it's getting late. It's one o'clock. Oh yer, we have something to tell you

Scruffy. We had to cross an enormous hole as deep as a house with water at the bottom to get here. We used an old VW door as a bridge, but it fell into the hole. Prancer tried jumping but nearly fell in so we can't go back that way. We have to find another way out," Chaffy said in a worried voice.

"The only way I can see out is through that hole in the ceiling. I could climb it then get help, but I will need a bunk up," offered Prancer.

Broozer, Maltliquor, and Chaffey helped Prancer up to the hole, then he grabbed a jagged rock and started to climb up the hole.

"ROOOOOOHRR."

"Quick Prancer," shouted Flyer, "the monster is coming back we have to hide."

Scruffy said, "Come over here, this is where I was hiding before you came."

"ROOOR, ROOOOR."

The monster came around the corner. They all saw it. It was enormous with big teeth. It was pure white all over and quite beautiful. Broozer took a picture on his phone and tried to send it, but there was no signal. Suddenly, they heard another noise.

"AHHHHHH!" Then there was a thump Prancer was lying in the green slime which cushioned his fall.

"Are you OK, Prancer?" whispered Maltliquor. There was no reply.

"Are you OK?" shouted Maltliquor.

"Yes, I think so," said Prancer gulping, looking up at four big eyes from the two babies, while gagging from the foul smell from the green slime. After checking that he has not hurt anything, Prancer quickly joined the rest of his friends. He pointed to the other end of the cave where there was a wide opening. The only trouble was that it was big enough for the monster to follow them. The Loch Ness monster didn't see the Six Macs. It made its way straight over to its babies where it started to lick them all over, licking off Broozer's scarf. After chewing it the monster spat it out with a snort.

"I think we should go for it. It could be the only way out," whispered Broozer.

"Bbbbut it could be a dddead-end," stammered Chaffy.

Maltliquor hissed open a can of Coca-Cola.

All of them said, "SHHHHH."

The monster quickly looked around, looking directly at them. "RUN, RUN, RUN," loudly shouted Broozer.

They all ran as fast as their legs could carry them. The monster roared and roared then came running after them. The floor was getting wetter and more slippery. It seemed to be going even steeper downhill. Broozer stopped for a second to get his breath back, shinning his torch towards the monster who didn't like the torch at all. It let out the biggest of all roars, which echoed all around the cave bouncing off every wall which deafened them all.

"That's interesting," shrieked Broozer, "it doesn't seem to like the torchlight. I'll see what happens if I shine it at its feet."

Broozer shone the torch at the monster's feet and it immediately started to come for them edging closer. He then shone it into its eyes, it roared and roared but stayed still shaking it head up and down with its tail flinging from side to side.

"That's it, if we all shine our torches into its eyes I think it will stop chasing us," instructed Broozer. So, they all shone their torches at the monster's eyes, which seemed to make it even angrier, but it didn't move.

Prancer shouted, "Smile Nessy," while taking a video, then quickly snapping a number of shots. Suddenly, Flyer slipped over, sliding down the wet slimy cold floor she slid out of view.

"ARRRRRRRrrrrrrrrrrrrrrrrr," screamed Flyer. They all tried to run after her, but all of them slipped over, tumbling and sliding down a very steep hill on their butts because their torches were no longer shining. It was very dark and the monster had started to chase them again. They all slid right into a large rock ending up in a pile. "Ooooo my head," shouted Flyer, as she pulled the boys up from the floor.

Prancer shone his torch around and, sure enough, it was a dead-end apart from the other side of the large rock where there was a very deep black hole with water splashing noises coming from it. "ARRR it's a dead end," screamed Maltliquor.

"It a good thing that the rock was there or all of us would have slid down the hole," shrieked Maltliquor.

"Wwwere ddddone for were going to be eeeeaten," squeaked Chaffy.

"Shine your torches," yelled Prancer.

"I can't find mine," shouted Chaffy.

"Nor me," screamed Flyer. In fact, Prancer was the only one left with a torch.

"It's down to you, Prancer, to save our lives," said Flyer. Prancer shone his torch at the monster, it roared but stayed in the same place.

"If we get out we are going to be famous. We're going to be on the front cover of all of the newspapers with Nessy," Scruffy proudly said.

"Or we may just end up in the monster's stomach," shuddered Maltliquor. Prancer lost his footing again, ending on the floor again. As he fell, his torch beam made something shine in the corner of the cave.

"Shine your torch over there again, Prancer," insisted Flyer. The monster roared then started to get closer as the torch started to get dimmer.

"Can you see over there? There's lots of white crystals, and look what's that opening next to them. Is it a small cave?" asked Scruffy.

"Quick Prancer shine your torch on the monster," shouted Maltliquor. They all slowly moved over to the opening in the side of the cave.

"It's a squeeze. You go first Prancer, shine your torch down the cave," insisted Scruffy. Just inside, it opened up to a larger cave, one at a time they all squeezed through the opening.

"Now, we are safe the monster can't get through that small hole. I think we should stop for ten minutes to eat our sandwiches I'm starving," begged Chaffy.

"Good idea, I'm starving too," agreed Flyer.

10. Rats

"I've got a surprise. My mum took it out of the deep freeze last night," Scruffy said, as he went into his bag.

"It's a large strawberry jam and cream sponge roll. Oh no! Look at this it's really quashed, and all the cream and jam has squished out inside my bag," he took out his hand, which was covered in a very sticky mess of yuckyness, "oooow, my hands really sticky. Does anyone want a lick?" joked Scruffy. They all shook their heads.

"I suppose that's a no," as he wiped his hand on his trousers.

Prancer's torch started to flicker as they finished their sandwiches, then with a brighter flicker Prancer's torch went out. Everything went totally black, so black that nothing could be seen. It was just like closing your eyes.

"That's done it," said Flyer taking out her phone from her pocket, putting the torchlight on.

"I don't think I have much juice left in my phone. How about you lot?" she said. In turn, they all said the same.

"I think we should now all turn off our phones except for Flyer. Then when her's runs out, we can use our's, one at a time," instructed Prancer. So, they all turned off their phones, the cave suddenly went rather dark with spooky shadows from stalactites on the cave walls that looked like ghostly figures. They could still hear the roar from the monster and were hoping it could not get to them through a different route. "ROOOOOR, ROOOOR," echoed the monster. Maltliquor chirped up.

"I know we have just eaten our sandwiches. But does anyone want a tin of coke?" They all swallowed in surprise.

"If you are offering," smiled Broozer.

"Here, I have four left. You can share them between you," Maltliquor said. So, they drank their can of Coca-Cola then started their way further down the cave which was still wet, damp, cold and very slippery. As they made their way further into the cave it started to get smaller and tighter. As Prancer squeezed through, he shouted back to the others, "It opens up down here."

Broozer was second and hoped the monster's egg would not get squashed, but he and the egg got through unscathed. Scruffy who was slightly fatter than the rest said, "I think I'm going to get stuck; I can't go any further, I'll get stuck."

"Come on, Scruffy squeeze. Hold your tummy in, I got through," yelled Maltliquor, who was also slightly overweight.

Scruffy held in his tummy and squeezed a bit more, "That's it. I'm stuck. I can't move. HELP! I'M STUCK, HELP!" he shouted.

"It opens up here, can you just squeeze another two metres? Then you will be OK I think I can hear water," shouted Prancer. Scruffy Squeezed and Squeeeeezed, and SQEEEEEEZED until he popped out the other end.

"You look like a flat gingerbread man," joked Broozer, as they all joyfully laughed, feeling very pleased with themselves that they had made it through the very tight gap and not having to have left Scruffy stuck in the cave. They rested a while before setting off further, surprisingly Flyer's torch on her phone was still quite bright as they trundled further down the cave.

They were all about one metre apart with Flyer at the front with Broozer at the back where it was quite dark.

"OOWW, what was that? **Sssomething bbbrushed pppas**t my ankle," screamed Chaffy, turning on his phone so that he could see what was on the floor. There to his horror and something that was **EEEEK** one of his worst fears, rats big fat juicy rats, they were everywhere.

"EEEEEK, Look on the floor, everyone," he shouted. They all turned on the phones to see what was nestling around their wellies.

"I don't mind rats. I used to have one as a pet. They're really clean animals and only bite when they're cornered," boasted Broozer.

Maltliquor and Prancer kept kicking them off their boots as they made it further down the cave. Chaffy was worried because he only had one boot, and he was afraid that a rat would bite one of his toes. To their surprise, there was a total dead-end apart from a hole about eighty-nine centimetres across full to the brim with water with a few rats and squiggly eel-like creatures swimming in the water. Prancer took a deep breath, then jumped into the hole of water and disappeared without telling anyone about his plan.

"Where's he gone?" cried Broozer.

"No idea, probably looking for a way out," answered Flyer. They all waited anxiously for Prancer's return.

"We have to go back I can't swim," panicked Maltliquor. Suddenly, there was a huge splash. Prancer come shooting up from the hole of water shouting.

"I've found a way out, all we have to do is swim for about one and a half metres then the cave opens up to a rocky ledge one metre above Loch Ness and only about forty metres away from the wood," he said all in one breath.

"You shouldn't just go off like that. You got all of us really worried, please don't do it again," asked Flyer. They all looked at Maltliquor MacSnigger.

"So, are you going to be the bravest coolest kid around ever? All you have to do is hold your breath for ten seconds," reassured Prancer, "the only trouble is, the pool is really deep. So, we will have to tie our scarves together then tie them around your waist. We can then pull you through the water to the other side."

Maltliquor went very quiet and looked rather pale. He pulled the ring from his very last can of drink.

"Arr! You still kept another one back," joked Flyer.

"Of course," said Maltliquor with a smug smile, then he went quiet again with a worried look on his face. He blurted out, "I'm not going down that hole, who would? Its wet, cold and black. There are rats, with lots of wiggly wormy things swimming around and it's WATER, **DEEPWATER** and I can't swim."

Chaffy looked at Flyer with a horrified look on his face.

"OOOOW! I forgot about the **ra-ra-ra-rats** with all of the excitement of **gggetting out of hhhhere,"** he gulped loudly. Prancer suggested he went first staying in the water on the other side of the watery tunnel to guide the others through. He jumped into the black hole of water and disappeared with a splash. Maltliquor and Chaffy looked with horror.

"We have to go for it, don't we?" sniffled Chaffy, who was feeling really cold and a bit shivery. His nose, now was constantly running and he had a bit of a sore throat. In all fairness, all of their noses were running from the dampness in the cave. Now they were about to get ringing wet, but the good thing was that it was warm and sunny outside. Flyer went next after taking a deep breath, SPLASH!

"She's gone, just like that," Broozer shouted, "here we go," then he was gone, with another SPLASH!

"So, who's going first?" asked Maltliquor.

"Not me," replied Chaffy, as a large brown rat crawled over his sock.

"I can't go, I can't swim," argued Maltliquor, not wanting to go at all. Broozer, unexpectedly, came out of the water hole holding one end of a scalf.

"Hi guys, I've come to help you through and I'm staying here until you two have swum through. So who's going first? Come on, one of you has to go because it's getting late and we'll all miss supper and be grounded for a week. Go on Chaffy! You go next, you can swim, just close your eyes then you won't see any rats, I'll go with you," assured Broozer.

Chaffy suddenly ran towards the dark hole, then with a splash, he disappeared into the wet void, forgetting to take his hat off, which floated to the top of the small pond. He found the other side in seconds, Prancer and Scruffy pulled him out of the water.

"There are no rats on this side, go outside and warm up," Scruffy happily said. Chaffy joined Flyer, who was shivering sitting on a rock above Loch Ness.

"It's warmer out here, but there's no way of telling the time my phone is soaked through," complained Flyer.

"Oh, I forgot about my phone, that means all of our phones are wet. Meaning they may not work again, meaning we have lost all of the pictures we took of the monster for the papers, meaning we won't be famous and have no proof of the Loch Ness monster. That sucks!" ranted Scruffy.

Back in the cave, Maltliquor was hovering over the hole. He had all of their scarves tied around his waist. Prancer had one end on the other side and Broozer had the other end.

"Go on, we have you," Prancer called the other two.

"Come and help me pull Maltliquor out. I think he may be coming through soon." All three waited anxiously hoping Maltliquor would appear, back on the other side. Maltliquor had his legs dangling in the water and it was pitch black because he had switched his phone off. Just at that moment they both heard a loud "ROOOOOOOOOR". With fright Maltliquor took a deep breath and jumped in, for him, it seemed to take hours and when he was only halfway through he felt a large rat brush past his nose. He panicked and opened his mouth taking in a large gulp of water. His arms were flapping which made it harder for Prancer to pull him through the water.

"Pull, Pull," shouted Prancer.

Prancer pulled him out using the scarves and Broozer pushed his legs out of the water. He was sputtering and splattering water out of his mouth.

He stood up then he joked, "Ooow that was cool," just to look brave, but really, he thought, he was going to drown. Hating the experience so much he thought, '*I never want to have a bath ever again.*'

They went outside.

Maltliquor asked, "What the time was?" After taking his phone out of his wet pocket then realising that his phone was wet and no longer working.

"We've ruined our phones," he complained.

"Yep, we have already worked that one out, also we've lost the monster's pictures," added Flyer.

"The monster's pictures mean we have no proof. It's just like when we found those gold coins then lost them and nobody believed us. They'll just say we have loads of imagination," fretted Scruffy, "well, we're out, and there's no sign of the monster."

11. The Monsters Return

All the boys took off their wet shirts. Flyer decided to keep her on.

"Let's slowly shuffle along this ledge but mind the rocks that are sticking out. They can be very slippery."

"You should stay between us so that you can hold on to us, so you don't fall into the Lock," instructed Prancer.

"Are you OK, Maltliquor?" asked Flyer.

"Yes, I think so," he nervously said.

"I can see the woods. We are nearly there," shouted Scruffy. As they made their way along the edge several times, each one of them nearly slipped into the Loch.

"Only another twenty metres, then we're safe," shouted Prancer. At that moment, a great big monster head came right out of the water, looking right at them with two big round eyes. It opened its mouth showing its long sharp teeth, then with a roooooor, splattered them with smelly green slime. They all froze stiller than a snowman on a frosty night.

Just as they thought nothing else could get worst. Prancer was the only one who did not freeze up. Instead, he had jumped further ahead, managing to get around a corner, to his horror. He saw something that would put Maltliquor into a panic. Meanwhile, Maltliquor was trying to balance on a tiny piece of rock, with now only Broozer holding one end of the scarf, which was tied around Maltliquor's waist. Nothing was said, there were no screams, no shouts for help with mouths open and eyes wide all five clung to the rocks with fear.

The monster gave one almighty **ROOOOAAAAAAAAAAAH,** then slipped back into the water. It was gone as quick as it had arrived. All five peeled themselves off the rocks. "Phew, that was a close one," screeched Scruffy. "It was as if it was saying goodbye or thank you for taking the hook out of one of the babies tails," sniffled Flyer. She was still pale from fright when she brushed the smelly green slime from her face which almost made her sick.

"Don't be silly, Flyer. I don't think monsters think like us," argued Broozer.

"There's no way that monster way saying goodbye," agreed Chaffy.

"It's more likely eyeing us up for its next meal. We've got to get off here as quick as possible. I think it's going to come back for supper. Don't forget we only saw one big monster if there are babies, there's got to be two or even four or five or ten or," exploded Maltliquor all in one breath.

"Oh, be quiet Maltliquor. You're scaring us all. I think it only eats fish and weeds and it won't be back," said Scruffy. At that point, Prancer came around the corner.

"You're not going to believe this, guys. The ledge just around the corner disappears into the water which is really deep. The woods are still about twenty metres away and this rock is too steep to climb up. So, we are going to have to swim for it."

Maltliquor looked at each one of the group and cried, "I CAN'T SWIM FOR IT. How am I going to get to the woods?"

"You could always wait here while we go off to get help," suggested Prancer. Maltliquor went quiet and started to think. "Well, what do you think? Do you want to stay here?" asked Prancer.

Maltliquor suddenly piped, "What if the monster comes back and eats me for supper?"

"Come with us then, we can all swim in a group holding you up, we can do this," encouraged Flyer holding her fist up. All the others touched fists in a line and shouted, "The Six Macs." They shouted again, "The Six Macs."

Smiling at each other, they continued along the edge until they got to the end. Prancer was first in the water which was freezing, all the others followed.

"OOOW it's cold," shouted Broozer.

"Ooooow, here comes the monster," joked Scruffy MacTuffy. Maltliquor then clung to the rocks. "Only joking," screamed Scruffy.

"Ooow I don't like this. You won't let me drown, will you?" whimpered Maltliquor, who was holding his mouth because his tooth was hurting again.

"Of course not," spluttered Prancer having just taken in a mouth full of water.

"Come on! Be brave jump in," Flyer said with chattering teeth. Maltliquor sat down on to his bottom with his legs dangling into the cold water then he slid into the water. They all made a raft out of their bodies then pulled Maltliquor on top of them making sure his head stayed well above the water. They then started to swim slowly towards the shore. Broozer still had not told his friends about the egg which made his bag float. As he was swimming, he started thinking that the monster may be looking for the egg which might put them all in danger.

They had only swum for about five metres when there was a massive swell in the water. Out of the deep came a huge white monster's head with a long neck, followed by a huge body with a great big white long tail. Brushing past them it almost tipped over their made-up body raft which was carrying Maltliquor.

"We are sitting ddducks. He's teasing us like a lion st, st, st, stalks his ppppprey before he eats it," stammered Chaffy.

"Maybe it's inquisitive like a dolphin, maybe it only wants to play," gurgled Flyer as she spat out a mouthful of water.

"Play, Play, you think it wants to play. With those big teeth, I think it's more likely to want to play who is for dinner tonight? Wooooo, here it comes again. Oooow don't drop me, will you?" shrieked Maltliquor.

"Arrrrh, I've got cramps in my legs because of this cold water. I'm sinking, ow, ow oow," cried Scruffy as he dropped away from his friends. Chaffy grabbed him before he sunk into the black deep water.

"Oww, ow, ow my leg, oow, ow. I can't swim, owww," griped Scruffy.

"There are only four swimmers now. This is really going to slow us down," screamed Flyer. The monster really made the biggest of all splashes. It splashed the water so much that it created a huge wave which pushed The Six Macs nearer to the shore. Then another huge splash followed by another huge wave pushing them even closer.

"The monster is helping us by making waves. If it wanted to eat us it has had loads of chances including the time it grabbed Scruffy in its mouth this morning," yelled Prancer.

"Oh no, here it comes again and I think it's coming at us faster than ever with its head underwater. I hope it hasn't got its mouth open. Oww glug, glug, oooooww," trembled Maltliquor. The monster hit the group with force scattering them, they all started to panic. Maltliquor splashed around for a while then slowly started to sink into the deep water. He was good at holding his breath because all of the Six Macs sometimes have had 'holding your breath' competitions.

As he went deeper and deeper he started to think that it might just be a dream, like Scruffy's dream and in a minute, he would wake up and bang his head on the table next to his bed. A panic feeling came over him knowing that after five-seconds he would not be able to hold his breath any longer and if it's not a dream he would drown. Only seconds had passed and he started panicking by splashing around.

Suddenly, he felt an arm grab him then another and another, then he felt the sensation of going up. As he hit the fresh air, he spat out loads of water, coughed and coughed then took an enormous breath of fresh air.

"I thought we had lost you," screamed Prancer.

"Cor that was scary," shivered Maltliquor, who was in total shock and was feeling very cold.

"Wow, you were lucky that water is really murky, we only just found you," cried Flyer.

"Yer' you were really lucky, mega, mega, lucky," squealed Scruffy, who's cramp had gone. They started swimming back to the land Prancer held Maltliquor under the chin holding his head up above the water, after only five minutes they were touching dry land.

12. Stinky Mud

"THANK YOU, THANK YOU, THANK YOU I made it, THANK YOU, I MADE IT, NO MORE MONSTERS," shouted Maltliquor excitingly.

They all stood up clenching their fists and shouted very loud, "THE SIX MACS."

"The heroes," added Maltliquor, who was feeling brave now that he was back on dry land.

"OOOOW I just saw the monster again. It's in the woods over there," pointed Broozer. They all went quiet. Prancer went to have a look. He cheered out loud, that's no monster it's one of the digger there, being used to dredge the river.

They all went into the wood and saw a giant digger with large grabbers that looked like big teeth.

"I think we should go and get my fishing rod before it gets any later," mentioned Maltliquor. So off they went, Chaffy's foot was feeling very sore from walking on all of the stones and rocks. He was now hobbling from a missing boot and he had to try not to stand on anything sharp.

"My dad's going to kill me for losing one of my boots. They were almost new. I got them as a birthday present," complained Chaffy.

"No, I don't think he will. Your da's nice when he finds out what happened to you I think he will let you off," assured Flyer.

"One good thing we don't have to go over that bridge we can just walk across the dry river bed," stated Scruffy. "There's the river," shouted Maltliquor, as he started running towards it and when he saw that it was empty of water. He jumped down the bank then to his surprise started to sink into the mud, which was on the river bed. It didn't stop at the top of his wellies nor did it stop at his knees nor his waist.

He shouted, **"HELP, HHHHHEEEELP, HELP**." The others arrived when it was up to his neck with his arms in the air, but he didn't seem to be sinking any further.

"Help me please! I don't want to sink any more, but I could because I think I'm standing on a wobbly stone," cried Maltliquor.

"That's what the diggers are for they must be getting out all of the mud as well," Broozer said, as he pointed to two more diggers. Prancer rushed over to retrieve the pole he had hidden under a bush that they had brought to retrieve Maltliquor's fishing rod from the water.

"Grab the pole Maltliquor," yelled Prancer. Maltliquor grabbed the pole then they all tugged at it pulling him out, but what a mess he was in. He was covered in black very, very stinky mud and his welly boots were totally full up with the gloopy stuff.

"Ha, you look funny, **oooooow** here comes the mud monster," chuckled Scruffy.

"You are going to spend hours in the bath tonight scrubbing that smell off," joked Scruffy.

"Oops we have a problem the only way back over the river from here is over that bridge. The last time I came over it some more wood fell into the water. I think it's about to collapse."

"We could go further down the bank then go over the bridge nearer to my fishing rod," suggested Maltliquor.

"No, we can't. It's a private wood in between here and the next bridge with high barbed-wire fences and someone told me that there are wild ferocious dogs roaming around eating people who trespass in the woods," explained Scruffy. By now, they had all warmed up from the warm sun that was shining down on them.

"So, it's the bridge," gasped Prancer.

"I have an idea," blurted Broozer, "I think we should collect as many long strong branches from the woods as we can, then sink them into the mud next to the bridge in three-metre gaps. We can then tie the branches against the bridge with ivy, that should make the bridge strong enough to get across. What do you think?"

"Fantastic idea, let's go for it, yes," cheered Scruffy, holding his arm in the air with his fist clenched then all the others followed and shouted, "The Six Macs."

So, off they went into the woods, after about half an hour they had collected enough wood for the job.

"Right then, I'll go first with this long one," said Prancer.

He stood carefully on the bridge then walked about two metres along one side. Then put the branch over the side pushing it into the thick squishy black mud.

"Ah, that's good. It's only half a metre deep here that should make it easier," Prancer pointed out. The bridge creaked, then it cheeked louder.

"Ooow, this may not work I can feel it moving, pass another piece of wood," shouted Prancer.

He then did the same on the other side carefully tying each branch to the bridge.

"Pass another branch Broozer. I'm happy to continue right across to the other side," instructed Prancer.

Each time he moved further across, it creaked and moaned as if to say I'm an old bridge and don't want to work anymore please let me fall on to the riverbed. After a while, Prancer had finished and was standing on the opposite side.

"WOW made it, come on you lot. I think it's safe to come over," bellowed Prancer, as he waved his arms in the air. Flyer went across first jumping over the holes.

"Woooow I felt it move, it's not very sturdy," claimed Flyer. Maltliquor had just managed to get most of the mud out of his wellies, but he still looked like a mud monster and he ponged.

He shouted over to Prancer and Flyer, "I don't want to end up in there again. Are you sure the bridge is safe?"

"I think it's safe enough for four more to get over, you should be OK."

Maltliquor was tired so he wasn't thinking straight, he just walked across. His fear seemed just to vanish before anyone could say anything, in fact, they were all speechless.

"There you go, easy, I did it, come on, your turn," boasted Maltliquor.

Chaffy started to hobble over when there was a giant creek then one side of the bridge just collapsed.

"ARRRH," he shouted, suddenly running and jumping with fear in his one boot until he got over to the opposite side. So only Scruffy and Broozer to go. They both decided to run over together.

They went into the woods then shouted as loud as they could, "HERE WE COME." They started to run as fast as they could, both jumping on the bridge at the same time. The bridge shuddered then as they ran across, it started to collapse behind them, falling into the squishy mud. They took one last leap on the bank before the bridge totally disintegrated into a pile of rotten wood on top of the mud. They both fell on the ground with surprise that they had made it.

"Now that's how it's done," screamed Broozer, laughing as the other patted him and Scruffy on their backs.

As they made their way along the bank they reminisced about their adventure.

"Wow, we've seen the Loch Ness monster, and its babies! Who gets to see baby monsters?" jeered Flyer.

"It's a shame we can't prove it with the selfies we took. Who is going to believe us?" groaned Scruffy.

"Cheer up, what a day even if no one believes us we know it was true," Prancer said in a cheery voice.

"Yer' our mums and dads will probably think we're making it up because I lost my boot and Broozer lost his scarf by putting it around the baby Loch Ness monster's tail," added Chaffy.

13. Honesty

"And how am I go'in to explain why I'm so muddy?" asked Maltliquor.

"My dad normally believes me. He'll go back with us to look for the monster," proclaimed Prancer.

"You're go' in back, ooow now way am I go' in back there, you'll get eaten for sure," shouted Maltliquor.

They arrived back were Maltliquor's rod was. The river bank was dry, sitting next to his rod was Bhreac Hoot's jacket wrapped around his fishing reel. Maltliquor slid down the bank. "Pass me the pole," requested Maltliquor.

He then leaned out, stretching his arms as far out as he could. The hook just reached the jacket which was really dirty and muddy. He pulled it back to the bank then grabbed his fishing rod which had a dead dried **trout on the hook.**

"Oooow I've caught a trout, **ooow** it's a bit stinky," as he took it off the hook.

"Poooo, my hands really stink now," Wiping them on the grass. Broozer picked up Bhreac Hoot's jacket.

"It's really heavy. I wonder what is in the pocket?" asked Broozer. As he went from pocket to pocket he found nothing then in a secret pocket on the inside of the jacket he felt something. "What have we here? I can feel money."

"Yes, it's my £2.41 p that he stole from me," said Maltliquor.

"No, there's more and a few £5 notes," panted Broozer. He counted all of the money £26.69p.

"Yes, we can go to the pictures tomorrow. Look at this lot Scruffy. We can go to the pictures."

"Don't forget there are Six Macs. We always share so divide it into six. I make it £4.10 something after paying Maltliquor's £2.41 back," teased Flyer then she said, "OK, you two can have the money to go to the pictures you can owe us."

"With all the cake I give you, I think I don't owe you anything," Scruffy added.

"True," Broozer nodded.

"I think we should put some rocks in Bhreac Hoot's jacket's pocket then throw it into the centre of the river, so it stays at the bottom. The Hoots will never know that the river was emptied," Chaffy suggested.

"But it may end up in one of those trucks after the river bed is dredged of mud," stressed Flyer.

"But they still won't know, they will still think it's at the bottom of the river after they fill it up again with water," added Broozer.

Prancer being the most sensible, had kept quiet.

"You are quiet Prancer," asked Broozer.

"Yes, I think it's wrong to keep the money probably the Hoots twins have stolen that money from kids at their school. I think we should give the money to Chaffy to give to his mum and dad, , because he goes to the same school as the Hoots. Then his dad can give the money to the headmaster. Twenty-six pounds sixty-nine pence is a lot of money."

"Your right Prancer, we should hand over the money. We're not thieves like the Hoots brothers," agreed Scruffy, even though he knew he would not be able to go to the pictures with his friends.

"So, do we all agree? We hand the money back?" asked Prancer. All of them agreed except Chaffy.

"Come on Chaffy, don't be a thief like the Hoots. You wouldn't like it if they had stolen from you, would you?" pleaded Scruffy.

"Oh, OK I agree. I will give the money to my dad. Give it here then, I will put it in my bag." He put the money carefully into his bag. They decided to put the Hoot's dirty shirt into a litter bin, because it was made of polyester, and it would probably pollute the river.

They then made their way back to their bikes after placing the long pole with the hook under a bush, just in case they needed it again. They are always pleased to see their bikes. It's a worry being away from them for so long. There's always a chance of them being stolen or vandalised. They put their torches back on their bikes, then took off at speed.

"I think we should go straight home, then we should all make it in time for supper," suggested Prancer.

So off they went home after such an adventure. When they got back all of them told their stories. That night all of the mums and dads phoned each other to discuss what the Six Macs had told them. Could it be true? Had they found the Loch Ness monster in a cave? They did express caution because the Six Macs were always telling stories of their adventures, which always sound a bit far-fetched. So, they all agreed to take a day off work the next day so that they can go and see if their story is true. After all, they all did come back soaking wet with all of their phones broken, and Chaffy did only have one boot.

Broozer sneaked his bag upstairs then took the monster's egg out from his bag. Carefully, he put it into the bottom of his cupboard wrapping it in his sleeping bag to keep it warm. Then started his screen time before bed, he began to think about having a Loch Ness monster for a pet, and taking it for walks on a leash. But because he was so tired, he fell fast asleep.

14. Disappointment

That morning the first thing all the mums did was to the phone the school, to explain what had happened at the weekend so that they could arrange for the Six Macs to take a day off school. Prancer's dad phoned the local newspaper. Then all of their parents told the Six Macs they had a surprise for them, it was that they were all going to the cave instead of going to school to look for the Loch Ness monster.

"That's no surprise, it's torture, I would rather go to school," grumbled Maltliquor to his dad. They all arrived at the car park next to the wood. The local newspaper reporter was waiting for them, a funny looking man with blue-rimmed glasses. In his ear there was a largish pink ear-ring, he had a grey beard and a slightly fat tummy. He wore a suit with a pink tie that matched Prancer's hair, which wasn't suitable for going down a cave.

"Hi Chaffy, my dad has brought along a wide ladder to get over the hole. I don't really want to do this, do you?" said Prancer.

"No, I'm really scared. No, I don't want to do this at all," answered Chaffy. The Six Macs went first showing their parents the way through the woods. After about twenty minutes of fighting their way through thick ferns they arrived at the fallen bridge.

"How are we going to get across the muddy river bed there's no bridge left?" asked Flyer. The river bed had filled up with quite a lot of water because it rained very heavy during the night. There was a fresh damp smell in the air with a mist dancing on ferns, which disappeared into the wood on the other side of the bridge.

Prancer's dad went for a walk then came back with a man driving a giant digger which was being used to dredge the riverbed. He shouted, "Boys and girls first, up you get, climb into the scooping bucket at the front of the digger," which was stinky with black wet mud.

"Ooow this is fun," said Flyer.

"Bit stinky, I spent one and a half hours in the bath scrubbing the smell off me from the mud last night. Now I'm going to have to do it all over again tonight," grumbled Maltliquor.

"It's not that muddy. Here, sit on my knees," insisted Flyer. So, when all were squashed into the bucket, the driver pulled a lever and up they went with a click, click, click, then forward. The arm of the digger stretched forward reaching right over the river bed to the other side. It then went down rather quickly with a BUMP, which made all of them shoot into the air, came down with another BUMP.

"OOOW that hurt my butt," complained Chaffy. They all climbed out.

"Your right Flyer. It's not that muddy just stinky," said Chaffy, as he scrapped a lump of smelly mud of his trousers. Then it was their parent's turn.

"First with four of you, then three at a time," shouted the driver who was a short man with spiky ginger hair.

"Go, careful driver. We don't want to go down with another bump, do we," shouted Maltliquor's mum. The driver wasn't a very friendly man. All he wanted was to get back to dredging the river, so he started driving faster and faster. It was the last journey. It was Chaffy's mum, Broozer's mum, and Dad's turn. They were three quarters away across when the driver made a silly mistake by pulling the wrong lever. It was the lever that tips out.

Suddenly there was a loud shout from Broozer's dad, "WAAAAAARRR."

Then a loud scream from Chaffy's mum, "SKREEEEEEEAAAAAAMMMM," as all three of them were tipped into the thick, smelly dark black deep mud. It wasn't very deep next to the bank, but they all piled in on top of each other.

"Are you alright, Mum?" shouted Chaffy.

"Yuk, I think so, this mud is so smelly," screamed Chaffy's mum. All three climbed up the bank.

"Cor, you all look like bog monsters," chuckled Broozer.

The Six Macs all looked at each other in amazement. Then all at the same time burst out in laughter. Maltliquor laughed so much this time he did wet his shorts but just only a bit before running off behind a tree to take wee.

All the way up to the cave, Broozer and Chaffy kept joking and teasing their parents about how they smelt by holding their noses and saying, "POOOOOOO." At the entrance of the cave, they all decided to sit down to have a late morning picnic, drinking Coca-Cola and eating chocolate cake. Flyer insisted that the parents covered in mud sat further away from them because they stank so much.

After half an hour, Flyer's da said, "Right then, let's go hunting Loch Ness monsters." They all cautiously started walking into the cave.

"BOOOO," shouted Prancer. They all jumped.

"That's not funny, it's getting an old joke you done that yesterday. It's just not funny you'll scare my mum," complained Flyer. They arrived at the hole, which was almost filled up with water from the rain the previous night, making it look like an intimidating pool of water.

"So, where's the deep nasty hole that the VW door fell down? There's just a little pool of water here," Broozer's dad joked.

"That hole is as deep as a house. This is where Chaffy fell in and nearly died," sighed Maltliquor. The mums and dads looked at each other as if to say, "Yer, yer, scary story. We don't think so, maybe you made up the first part of the story just to make your adventure sound more exciting." The newspaperman took a picture of the pool saying in a sarcastic voice, "Oow how exciting." Prancer's dad put the ladder across the pool of water. The adults just walked across with no fear whatsoever, one step then over. The Six Macs felt a little more nervous crossing, because they knew the pool really was as deep as a house. They continued down the slippery path. The cave was dripping droplets of freezing cold water on to their heads from the stalactites that hung from its ceiling.

There was a spooky eeriness just like the day before, but something was missing. There were no **ROOOOORS.** All that could be heard was dripping sounds, and footsteps from their boots. They went further into the cave. The Six Macs were all nervous, expecting the monster to come up towards them roaring and showing its big teeth.

After a slippery walk, they arrived at the place where the baby monsters were but there was no sign of the babies. In fact, the slimy place where they were was clean with spring water. Because it had been raining, there was a waterfall gushing out of the ceiling then cascading down on to where the baby monsters were.

The water had washed away all of the smelly slime turning the pool into a freshwater pond.

"So, where are the baby monsters?" asked the reporter.

"They were here, just here, we took selfies with them. I took out a fishing hook from one of the baby monster's tail then wrapped it with my scarf," explained Broozer, as he scratched his head.

"Look, Broozer, there's your scarf over there. I'll get it," offered Scruffy. Scruffy picked up the wet scarf on it was a green smelly slime.

"Here you are, Dad, smell this, we are telling the truth, we are, aren't we Prancer?" insisted Chaffy.

"Yes, Dad, we are all telling the truth," answered Prancer. "That's just slimy weed. Look it's around everywhere," jeered Broozer's dad.

All of the parents were disappointed, so they started walking back up the slippery slope out of the cave, followed by the Six Macs. They went back over the pool.

"It's a fantastic cave," said Flyer's da, as they were leaving.

"Ooooh that sun's bright," said Chaff's dad, as they all squinted.

"Another wasted morning, I can't tell you how many wasted mornings I've have had over the last twenty years. Loch Ness monster here, Loch Ness monster there, Loch Ness monster everywhere, but THERE NEVER IS ONE," the reporter shouted with anger.

"How are we going to get back over the riverbed? The man who uses the digger will be busy dredging the riverbank," asked Flyer's mum.

"I go fishing on the Loch, I have a boat moored up right down the hill on the other side of those rocks. If we row along the edge of the loch there's a lifeboat station that we can row to, which is nowhere near the river. From there we can get a lift to our cars," answered Prancer's dad.

He was talking about the same rocks on which the Six Macs sat looking over Loch Ness before going into the cave the day before. The Six Macs really weren't sure about going on a boat knowing the monster was swimming around.

They climbed down a rocky steep path with the odd muddy puddle which housed sharp spiky bracken. It scratched their legs as they brushed past it. There was a damp, slimy weed smell that rose up from the water below, that reminded them of the slime inside the cave where the baby Loch Ness monsters were.

"Cccccan, you ssssssmell that?" asked Chaffy Mactaff.

"Yes, it smells like the cave and like the slime," answered Maltliquor MacSnigger.

"Ooooow, I'm nnnot sure about this bbbboat thing," stammered Chaffy.

"Come on you lot, get a move on," boomed Broozer's dad from the bottom of the hill.

"Come on Maltliquor, another adventure," said Prancer.

"I don't want another adventure, especially if it has anything to do with the Loch Ness monster," complained Maltliquor. They all arrived at the bottom of the hill. All of the mums and dads were already in the boat, which was old and rickety but big enough for all of them to sit in comfortably, it even had two sets of oars. The Macs climbed into the boat which wobbled from side to side.

"Here you are, Maltliquor put this life jacket on. It will make you feel safer," said Prancer.

15. A Monster Ride

There was a slight breeze with quite a thick mist resting on the water. With the warm sun above trying to break through, the visibility wasn't very good.

Maltliquor, Chaffy, Flyer and Broozer's dads took an oar each while Prancer's dad took the udder to steer the boat. The water was still. All that could be heard was the splash of the oars as they cut through the water.

"Are we going the right way?" asked Prancer's mum.

"I'm not too sure. I've never been on the loch when it has been misty before. The warm sun should burn off the mist soon so that we can see, but if we are going the right way, we should be there in ten minutes," answered Prancer's dad.

Ten minutes later, they were still rowing and feeling a bit anxious. The mist was still very thick; in fact, it was getting thicker and thicker.

"I think the mmmmist is getting thicker, and it's also ggggetting colder," cried Chaffy.

"Hey Dad, I think where going the wrong way because it's getting colder, I think we should turn around," suggested Prancer MacDancer.

Suddenly, a great big white monster's body swept silently past their boat, causing a giant wave almost tipping the boat over. As it passed, it broke two of the oars while pushing Flyer's and Broozer's dads off their seats. The newspaper reporter fell backwards, throwing his camera accidentally into the Loch.

The camera sank into the deep water.

"What was that? What was that?" shouted the reporter.

"Did you see that?" shrieked Flyer's mum.

"See, we were telling the truth it was the Loch Ness monster," answered Prancer. At that point, the mist started to clear. They all looked around, they were right in the middle of the loch, and the land was rather a long way away.

Broozer started to think that if he hadn't stolen the egg, just maybe the monster would not have been chasing them but couldn't say anything.

"We are all going to be eaten," shouted the reporter, who wished he had kept his camera on a strap around his neck. The water went still again. The eerie mist swirled on the water from the light breeze. Everyone in the boat was very quiet as they were all terrified, not wanting to make a noise just in case the monster came back.

"SHHHhhhh," whispered Chaffy's dad.

All the mums and dads had their smart phones out ready to take pictures. They all had tried to phone for help, but there was no signal on the Loch.

Prancer's dad said, "Pull one of the oars over to the other side so that we can start to row to the lifeboat station."

"We have to get going. We can't stay here were like sitting ducks," insisted Broozer's mum.

So, off they went. In the distance about four hundred metres away, they could see what looked like a white hump sticking out of the water. Which made them row faster.

They were nearing the bank and were feeling quite relaxed that the monster had not come back. When suddenly, there was an almighty SPLASH. All of the mums and dads were still holding the phones, who got such a fright that they threw their smart phones into the air. All their phones splashed into the water. They all looked at each other in fear of their lives.

"The mmmmonster is under the bbbbboat," stammered Chaffy. Slowly, the monster lifted the boat upon it's back high up, and out of the water tipping the boat to one side. Hurling them all into the water with a SPLASH. Except Flyer's mum who caught her novelty bracelet on one of the monsters hooked horns, which were on the back off its neck. The monster then dived back into the water and disappeared into the deep, with Flyer's mum attached to its neck.

Flyer's mum was called Penny. If anyone had been chosen to get attached to the monster, Penny was the best person. She was a scout leader, and held swimming classes at the local school. Her speciality was to swim underwater without coming up for air for a whole length of the swimming pool.

Everybody was panicking, slashing and swishing around in the water.

"Where's my son Maltliquor? He can't swim," shouted Maltliquor's dad.

"Here I am. Help me. Help," spluttered Maltliquor.

He was bobbing around in the water with his arms flapping around like a swan in a pond. His head was just above the water and he was spitting and spurting water out of his mouth.

"Help, Dad, help me, I'm over here, help me, Dad," Maltliquor shouted. It was a good job Maltliquor had a life jacket on or he would have certainly drowned.

They all managed to get back into the boat. All wet, all bedraggled, disorientated, splattering, spluttering and all quite scared. Flyer and her da looked at each other. There was someone missing.

"Where's Mum?" shouted Flyer. They both looked over the boat. She was nowhere to be seen.

"MUM, MUM, MUM," shouted Flyer.

"PENNY, PENNY, PENNY, PENNY. She's the best swimmer here, where is she?" sniffled Flyer's da.

The loch was still again. Flyer started to cry.

"We couldn't have lost Mum. Where is she, Da? Where is she?" cried Flyer. She had a dreadful thought that her mum had been eaten by the Loch Ness monster, and she would never ever see her mum again. The boat started to rock again. They all quickly grabbed each other. The Six Macs held their parent's shaky hands tightly who seemed more scared than they did.

The monster rose out of the deep and roared loudly, but something was different this time. Riding on its neck like someone riding a horse was Flyer's mum with one arm in the air so that she could balance on its slender neck. As the monster started to go back into the water, Flyer's mum slid down its smooth white neck into the water. Then the monster was gone. Penny swam to the boat and they all pulled her in.

"WOW, that was the best ride I have ever had. My bracelet caught around its neck, and it pulled me underwater, but it needs air, so I only had to hold my breath for a little while. I stayed on its back hoping that it would come back here. I think it is just curious like a dolphin. I don't think it eats people. It just eats fish and green slimy weed. That's why its breath smells of rotten fish, so I wasn't scared. It lives in a cave right under this boat, so we have to row away from this area to stop it from lifting the boat up out of the water again." explained Penny.

"That's why Flyer is a daredevil on her state board. She's a brave Scot like her mum," shouted Scruffy.

They quickly started to row back before the monster returned. The boat was half full of water which came up to their waists. With only two oars they couldn't go fast at all. As they rowed, the water kept rippling around them as if the monster was swimming underwater around the boat. This made them all very nervous.

Eventually, they arrived at the lifeboat station with no pictures of evidence, no mobile phones, clothes ringing wet and feeling very cold.

"I'm not going to write an article in the newspapers tomorrow because I have no pictures. When I get pictures, I will write the biggest story ever. That day will come I know it. If I write just an article with no pictures, it will be like other stories. Nessy has been seen again but nobody believes the stories any-more," said the journalist.

Prancer's dad hooked up the boat. They were all cold and shivering. Prancer's dad went to find someone to give them a lift back to their cars but could not find a single person.

"We're going to have to walk back. I think it will take about an hour," said Prancer's dad in an exhausted voice.

By the time they got back, most of their clothes were dry from the warm sun. The Six Macs sneaked behind some bushes so their parents could not see them, they quickly clenched their fists then shouted, "The Six Macs," then one by one left to go home. Nobody really felt like talking much on the way home. Their mums and dads were still in shock after what had just happened.

16. The Right Thing to Do

The first thing Broozer did when he got home was to see if the egg had hatched which it had not. Then he started to think what would happen if it did hatch. How would he feed a baby Loch Ness monster? But then thought it would be proof that the monster existed which would be far better than a picture. He was just about to go downstairs to tell his mum and dad about the egg when the house telephone rang, his mum shouted, "It's for you Max." Broozer's real name was Max.

"Hi, it's me Prancer. I think really, it's a good thing that we didn't get pictures of the monster, and the newspaperman has decided not to print a story. Just imagine if we had got pictures of proof, the next thing would be that there would be loads of scientists turning up with nets and cages, then they would take the Loch Ness monsters away to put them in zoos. So, there wouldn't be Loch Ness monsters any more. Also, television people and news reporters, from all over the world hundreds of them would be interviewing us, and trampling all over our woods spoiling them. I've spoken to the others we've decided to make a pact," explained Prancer.

"What type of pact?" asked Broozer.

"We will have to touch fist to seal the pact next time we meet, but this is it. We will never tell anyone about what we saw. We have to keep Nessy monster Scottish by protecting them so that they can swim freely in the Lock forever. Are you in?" asked Prancer.

"Well. Yes," hesitated Broozer, thinking of the egg.

"All of the other mums and dads are going for it as well," continued Prancer. They both said, "Goodbye."

Broozer went back upstairs he looked at the egg. He thought to himself, '*How am I going to get it back to the cave? With it being school tomorrow and how am I going to cross the river with no bridge?*' He had his shower then went to bed and immediately fell asleep. The next morning, he woke to loud noise in his bedroom. He jumped up straight to where the egg was. He shook his head to wake up properly only to find his dad banging on his door.

"Come on, get up, school time."

He brushed his teeth then got dressed.

There was no way he could miss school today. He had a football match against Chaffy's school, he thought, as he walked downstairs.

"Loch Ness monster on toast," joked his mum. Chaffy rolled his eyes.

"That's an old joke Mum, ha-ha."

After breakfast, he went upstairs to check the cupboard, crossing his fingers. He pulled back the curtains then opened up the sleeping bag, hoping that the egg had not hatched. "Phew," he whispered. It was still whole. He carefully stroked it then suddenly felt something tap on the shell from the inside. He jumped back. Then thought, '*I just have to chance it.*'

He carefully zipped up the sleeping bag then went off to school. After school, Broozer forgot about the egg because he was feeling thrilled. His football team had thrashed Chaffy's school 10–1 and as a special treat for what had happened on the Loch the day before, all of the Six Mac's mums and dads had clubbed together to treat them all by giving them enough money to go the pictures, buy a burger, popcorn and drinks of pop. They all met at the pictures Jade and Emma were waiting there too.

"Oww this is a bit of treat for a Monday, I can't wait to see the film. Before going in, we have to seal the pact about Nessy," smiled Flyer. They clenched their fists and shouted, "Keep Nessy Monster Scottish."

"So, can we join your little gang?" teased Jade.

"No, the eight Mac's doesn't sound right," shouted Chaffy, who didn't really know the two girls.

"Only joking, no need to get your pants in a twist," teased Jade. The pact reminded Broozer of the egg who thought about it for about three minutes before going back to enjoyment mode.

The next morning, Broozer woke up early and thankfully the egg was still whole. He carefully put the monster's egg into his school bag then went down for his breakfast. His mum said, "I will put your packed lunch in your bag." Broozer jumped up out of his chair.

"It's all right, Mum, I will put them into my bag," He carefully put the bag over his shoulders then started to cycle to school. Upon arriving there, he cycled right past the school and continued down the hill heading to the river. He decided to cycle through the woods, carefully avoiding any deep rabbit or badger holes. At the river, his luck was in, the people who were dredging the river weren't there. The water had been put back, and there was a small boat moored against the riverbank that they had been using. He climbed into the boat sitting down onto a wooden seat.

It was raining quite hard, making the seat on the boat wet, which soaked through to his underpants and made his trousers feel very uncomfortable and cold. He rowed upriver getting off where the broken bridge was, he tied the boat to a tree, then started walking up the hill towards the cave. At the cave, he hesitated before going inside. He was extremely scared as he shone his torch, the shadows seemed a lot bigger. It seemed spookier than he remembered. He arrived at the hole still full of water.

Broozer heard a loud Rooooor, he leapt back with fright, landing on a small rock twisting his ankle. He tried to stand up. "Ow, ow that hurts I can't walk, what now?" he whispered to himself. He took the egg carefully out of his bag to check that he had not smashed it when he tripped over, but it was fine. He put the egg carefully onto the ground then started to crawl up the slope on his hands and knees. He found it hard because he also had to hold the torch.

He heard another "ROOOOR". He shined his torch towards the rooooar.

Almost immediately, a monster came out of the dark. It roared then picked the egg up in its mouth then sped off further back into the cave.

"Wow, that's it, no more monsters forever and ever," he vowed.

He crawled to the side of the cave, levering himself up against the wall then started to hobble back out of the cave. Then unexpectedly, the ground began to rumble. He shone his torch into the cave and to his amazement, two Loch Ness monsters, one slightly bigger, were heading straight for him.

To his amazement, the bigger one stopped while the smaller one continued to walk towards him. Broozer was frozen with fear. Then it sniffed his head before giving of a loud sneeze which covered him in green smelly slime. It sniffed him again, then started to walk back down into the dark cave with its mate. Broozer couldn't believe it, he was relieved that he wasn't eaten. Broozer had a strange idea that the monster had covered him in smelly slime as a punishment for steeling its egg.

He managed to crawl back to the entrance, where he phoned for help on a phone he had borrowed from his sister.

Broozer couldn't believe it, in just five minutes a helicopter buzzed over his head before landing forty metres away.

"Hello, what do we have here? And what are you doing here all by yourself? Shouldn't you be at school?" Asked a man with a helmet and a high vis orange jacket.

Broozer had to think quick.

"I'm doing a project on slow worms, and I thought this place would be the best place to find them," lied Broozer.

"Well, I think in future you should look a little nearer to your school. You need to go to hospital with that ankle. POOOOO, you smell nasty, you're going to smell our helicopter out. Why are you covered in smelly slime?" Asked the man.

"Oh, fell into a stagnant pond by mistake," lied Broozer.

Broozer had never been in a helicopter before, so he really enjoyed the ride. He noticed the pilot was holding his nose. At the hospital, he found out that he had broken his ankle, so it had to be put into plaster. When his mum and dad picked him up, he told them his story.

"We are very proud of you, you did the right thing returning the egg," smiled Broozer's dad.

Once home, the other five Macs were waiting for him, Broozer's parents had invited them for supper. In turn, they wrote their real names on Broozer's plaster cast, then shouted, "THE SIX MACS."